Dear Reader,

There has never been a magical kingdom quite like Oz. Populated by good witches and wicked witches, wretched Nomes and enchanting princesses, chattering hens and cowardly lions—a whole host of marvelous creatures great and small and wise and wonderful—Oz is one of the most beloved fantasy worlds ever created.

The enormous explosion of all types of fantasy that we are seeing in today's market makes us feel that now is the time for a brilliantly successful Oz revival.

When we mention Oz to people who haven't grown up with the books, they nod, mention Judy Garland and think they know all there is to know about Oz. How wrong they are! They have no idea how rich the series is, how many wonderful characters and creatures there are. We have every expectation of making Oz as familiar to millions of fantasy readers as is Tolkien's Middle-earth and Lewis's Narnia.

Del Rey Books is now publishing the original fourteen Baum Oz books.

Come, join us in Oz.

Magically,
Judy-Lynn & Lester del Rey
Del Rey Books

 **IS . . .**

"Oz—where the young stay young and the old grow young forever—these books are for readers of all ages."
    —Ray Bradbury

"Who says the Land of Oz is only for the young? Age has nothing to do with it. Oz belongs to the young at heart and always will. All that is needed is an adventuresome spirit and a genuine affection for classic fantasy."
    —Terry Brooks
        Author of *The Sword of Shannara*

"I was raised with the Oz books, and their enchantment, humor and excitement remain with me. They are still a joy and a treasure. I welcome this Oz revival."
    —Stephen R. Donaldson
        Author of *The Chronicles of Thomas Covenant*

"The land of Oz has managed to fascinate each new generation . . . the Oz books continue to exert their spell . . . and those who read [them] are often made what they were not—imaginative, tolerant, alert to wonders, life."
    —Gore Vidal
        The New York Review of Books

THIS BOOK BELONGS TO

DANIEL BROWN

The Wonderful Oz Books by L. Frank Baum
Now Published by Del Rey Books

RINKITINK
IN OZ

Wherein is recorded the Perilous Quest of
Prince Inga of Pingaree and King
Rinkitink in the Magical
Isles that lie beyond
the Borderland
of Oz.

BY

L. FRANK BAUM

"Royal Historian of Oz"

ILLUSTRATED BY

JOHN R. NEILL

A Del Rey Book

BALLANTINE BOOKS · NEW YORK

Copyright 1916
By L.Frank Baum

ALL RIGHTS
RESERVED

A Del Rey Book
Published by Ballantine Books

"The Marvelous Land of Oz" Map copyright © 1979 by James
E. Haff and Dick Martin. Reproduced by permission of The
International Wizard of Oz Club, Inc.

Published in the United States by Ballantine Books, a division
of Random House, Inc., New York, and simultaneously in
Canada by Random House of Canada Limited, Toronto, Canada.

Library of Congress Catalog Card number: 77-089296

ISBN 0-345-33317-9

This edition published by arrangement with Contemporary
Books, Inc.

Manufactured in the United States of America

First Ballantine Books Edition: November 1980
Third Printing: August 1985

Cover art by Michael Herring

To
My New Grandson~
Robert Alison Baum

Introducing this Story

Here is a story with a boy hero, and a boy of whom you have never before heard. There are girls in the story, too, including our old friend Dorothy, and some of the characters wander a good way from the Land of Oz before they all assemble in the Emerald City to take part in Ozma's banquet. Indeed, I think you will find this story quite different from the other histories of Oz, but I hope you will not like it the less on that account.

If I am permitted to write another Oz book it will tell of some thrilling adventures encountered by Dorothy, Betsy Bobbin, Trot and the Patchwork Girl right in the Land of Oz, and how they discovered some amazing creatures that never could have existed outside a fairyland. I have an idea that about the time you are reading this story of Rinkitink I shall be writing that story of Adventures in Oz.

Don't fail to write me often and give me your advice and suggestions, which I always appreciate. I get a good many letters from my readers, but every one is a joy to me and I answer them as soon as I can find time to do so.

L. Frank Baum
Royal Historian of Oz

"OZCOT"
at HOLLYWOOD
in CALIFORNIA
1916.

LIST OF CHAPTERS

xi

IMPASSABLE

The MARVELOU

GILLIKIN

WINKIE

COUNTRY

QUADLING

DEADLY DESERT

GREAT SAN

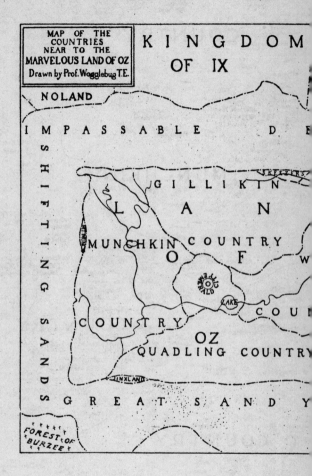

MAP OF THE
COUNTRIES
NEAR TO THE
MARVELOUS LAND OF OZ
Drawn by Prof. Wogglebug T.E.

KINGDOM
OF IX

NOLAND

IMPASSABLE   D   E

SHIFTING

GILLIKIN
S.KEIZER'S

L   A   N

MUNCHKIN   COUNTRY

O   F   W

EMERALD
CITY

LAKE

SANDS

COUNTRY

COU

OZ

QUADLING COUNTRY

INXLAND

GREAT SANDY Y

FOREST
OF
BURZEE

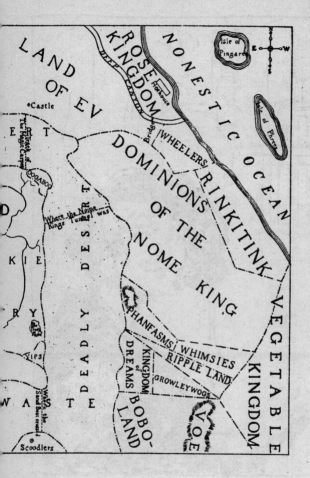

The Prince of Pingaree

CHAPTER 1

IF you have a map of the Land of Oz handy, you will find that the great Nonestic Ocean washes the shores of the Kingdom of Rinkitink, between which and the Land of Oz lies a strip of the country of the Nome King and a Sandy Desert. The Kingdom of Rinkitink isn't very big and lies close to the ocean, all the houses and the King's palace being built near the shore. The people live much upon the water, boating and fishing, and the wealth of Rinkitink is gained from trading along the coast and with the islands nearest it.

Four days' journey by boat to the north of Rinkitink is the Island of Pingaree, and as our story begins here I must tell you something about this island. At the north end of Pingaree, where it is widest, the land is a mile from shore to shore, but at the south end it is scarcely half a mile broad; thus, although Pingaree is four miles long, from north to south, it cannot be called a very big island. It is exceedingly pretty, however, and to the gulls who approach it from the sea it must resemble a huge green wedge lying upon the waters, for its grass and trees give it the color of an emerald.

The grass came to the edge of the sloping shores; the beautiful trees occupied all the central portion of Pingaree, forming a continuous grove where the branches met high overhead and there was just space beneath them for the cosy houses of the inhabitants. These houses were scattered everywhere throughout the island, so that there was no town or city, unless the whole island might be called a city. The canopy of leaves, high overhead, formed a shelter from sun and rain, and the dwellers in the grove could all look past the straight tree-trunks and across the grassy slopes to the purple waters of the Nonestic Ocean.

At the big end of the island, at the north, stood the royal palace of King Kitticut, the lord and ruler of Pingaree. It was a beautiful palace, built entirely of snow-white marble and capped by domes of burnished gold, for the King was exceedingly wealthy. All along the coast of Pingaree were found the largest and finest pearls in the whole world.

These pearls grew within the shells of big oysters, and the people raked the oysters from their watery beds, sought out the milky pearls and carried them dutifully to their King. Therefore, once every year His Majesty was able to send six of his boats, with sixty rowers and many sacks of the valuable pearls, to the Kingdom of Rinkitink, where there was a city called Gilgad, in which King Rinkitink's palace stood on a rocky headland and served, with its high towers, as a lighthouse to guide sailors to the harbor. In Gilgad the pearls from Pingaree were purchased by the King's treasurer, and the boats went back to the island laden with stores of rich merchandise and such supplies of food as the people and the royal family of Pingaree needed.

The Pingaree people never visited any other land but that of Rinkitink, and so there were few other lands that knew there was such an island. To the southwest was an island called the Isle of Phreex, where the inhabitants had no use for pearls. And far north of Pingaree— six days' journey by boat, it was said—were twin islands named Regos and Coregos, inhabited by a fierce and warlike people.

Many years before this story really begins, ten big boatloads of those fierce warriors of Regos and Coregos visited Pingaree, landing suddenly upon the north end of the island. There they began to plunder and conquer, as was their custom, but the people of Pingaree, although neither so big nor so strong as their foes, were able to defeat them and drive them all back to the sea, where a great storm overtook the raiders from Regos and Coregos and destroyed them and their boats, not a single warrior returning to his own country.

This defeat of the enemy seemed the more wonderful because the pearl-fishers of Pingaree were mild and peaceful in disposition and seldom quarreled even among themselves. Their only weapons were their oyster rakes; yet the fact remains that they drove their fierce enemies from Regos and Coregos from their shores.

King Kitticut was only a boy when this remarkable battle was fought, and now his hair was gray; but he remembered the day well and, during the years that followed, his one constant fear was of another invasion of his enemies. He feared they might send a more numerous army to his island, both for conquest and revenge, in which case there could be little hope of successfully opposing them.

This anxiety on the part of King Kitticut led him to keep a sharp lookout for strange boats, one of his men patrolling the beach constantly, but he was too wise to allow any fear to make him or his subjects unhappy. He was a good

King and lived very contentedly in his fine palace, with his fair Queen Garee and their one child, Prince Inga.

The wealth of Pingaree increased year by year; and the happiness of the people increased, too. Perhaps there was no place, outside the Land of Oz, where contentment and peace were more manifest than on this pretty island, hidden in the bosom of the Nonestic Ocean. Had these conditions remained undisturbed, there would have been no need to speak of Pingaree in this story.

Prince Inga, the heir to all the riches and the kingship of Pingaree, grew up surrounded by every luxury; but he was a manly little fellow, although somewhat too grave and thoughtful, and he could never bear to be idle a single minute. He knew where the finest oysters lay hidden along the coast and was as successful in finding pearls as any of the men of the island, although he was so slight and small. He had a little boat of his own and a rake for dragging up the oysters and he was very proud indeed when he could carry a big white pearl to his father.

There was no school upon the island, as the people of Pingaree were far removed from the state of civilization that gives our modern children such advantages as schools and learned professors, but the King owned several manuscript books, the pages being made of sheepskin.

Being a man of intelligence, he was able to teach his son something of reading, writing and arithmetic.

When studying his lessons Prince Inga used to go into the grove near his father's palace and climb into the branches of a tall tree, where he had built a platform with a comfortable seat to rest upon, all hidden by the canopy of leaves. There, with no one to disturb him, he would pore over the sheepskin on which were written the queer characters of the Pingarese language.

King Kitticut was very proud of his little son, as well he might be, and he soon felt a high respect for Inga's judgment and thought that he was worthy to be taken into the confidence of his father in many matters of state. He taught the boy the needs of the people and how to rule them justly, for some day he knew that Inga would be King in his place. One day he called his son to his side and said to him:

"Our island now seems peaceful enough, Inga, and we are happy and prosperous, but I cannot forget those terrible people of Regos and Coregos. My constant fear is that they will send a fleet of boats to search for those of their race whom we defeated many years ago, and whom the sea afterwards destroyed. If the warriors come in great numbers we may be unable to oppose them, for my people are little trained to fighting at best; they surely would cause us much injury and suffering."

"Are we, then, less powerful than in my grandfather's day?" asked Prince Inga.

The King shook his head thoughtfully.

"It is not that," said he. "That you may fully understand that marvelous battle, I must confide to you a great secret. I have in my possession three Magic Talismans, which I have ever guarded with utmost care, keeping the knowledge of their existence from anyone else. But, lest I should die and the secret be lost, I have decided to tell you what these talismans are and where they are hidden. Come with me, my son."

He led the way through the rooms of the palace until they came to the great banquet hall. There, stopping in the center of the room, he stooped down and touched a hidden spring in the tiled floor. At once one of the tiles sank downward and the King reached within the cavity and drew out a silken bag.

This bag he proceeded to open, showing Inga that it contained three great pearls, each one as big around as a marble. One had a blue tint and one was of a delicate rose color, but the third was pure white.

"These three pearls," said the King, speaking in a solemn, impressive voice, "are the most wonderful the world has ever known. They were gifts to one of my ancestors from the Mermaid Queen, a powerful fairy whom he once had the

good fortune to rescue from her enemies. In gratitude for this favor she presented him with these pearls. Each of the three possesses an astonishing power, and whoever is their owner may count himself a fortunate man. This one having the blue tint will give to the person who carries it a strength so great that no power can resist him. The one with the pink glow will protect its owner from all dangers that may threaten him, no matter from what source they may come. The third pearl—this one of pure white—can speak, and its words are always wise and helpful."

"What is this, my father!" exclaimed the Prince, amazed; "do you tell me that a pearl can speak? It sounds impossible."

"Your doubt is due to your ignorance of fairy powers," returned the King, gravely. "Listen, my son, and you will know that I speak the truth."

He held the white pearl to Inga's ear and the Prince heard a small voice say distinctly: "Your father is right. Never question the truth of what you fail to understand, for the world is filled with wonders."

"I crave your pardon, dear father," said the Prince, "for clearly I heard the pearl speak, and its words were full of wisdom."

"The powers of the other pearls are even greater," resumed the King. "Were I poor in all else, these gems would make me richer than any other monarch the world holds."

"I believe that," replied Inga, looking at the beautiful pearls with much awe. "But tell me, my father, why do you fear the warriors of Regos and Coregos when these marvelous powers are yours?"

"The powers are mine only while I have the pearls upon my person," answered King Kitticut, "and I dare not carry them constantly for fear they might be lost. Therefore, I keep them safely hidden in this recess. My only danger lies in the chance that my watchmen might fail to discover the approach of our enemies and allow the warrior invaders to seize me before I could secure the pearls. I should, in that case, be quite powerless to resist. My father owned the magic pearls at the time of the Great Fight, of which you have so often heard, and the pink pearl protected him from harm, while the blue pearl enabled him and his people to drive away the enemy. Often have I suspected that the destroying storm was caused by the fairy mermaids, but that is a matter of which I have no proof."

"I have often wondered how we managed to win that battle," remarked Inga thoughtfully. "But the pearls will assist us in case the warriors come again, will they not?"

"They are as powerful as ever," declared the King. "Really, my son, I have little to fear from any foe. But lest I die and the secret be lost to the next King, I have now given it into your keeping. Remember that these pearls are the rightful heritage of all Kings of Pingaree. If at any time I should be taken from you, Inga, guard this treasure well and do not forget where it is hidden."

"I shall not forget," said Inga.

Then the King returned the pearls to their hiding place and the boy went to his own room to ponder upon the wonderful secret his father had that day confided to his care.

The Coming of King Rinkitink

CHAPTER 2

A few days after this, on a bright and sunny morning when the breeze blew soft and sweet from the ocean and the trees waved their leaf-laden branches, the Royal Watchman, whose duty it was to patrol the shore, came running to the King with news that a strange boat was approaching the island.

At first the King was sore afraid and made a step toward the hidden pearls, but the next moment he reflected that one boat, even if filled with enemies, would be powerless to injure him, so he curbed his fear and went down to the beach to discover who the strangers might be. Many of the men of Pingaree assembled there also, and Prince Inga followed his father. Arriving at the water's edge, they all stood gazing eagerly at the oncoming boat.

It was quite a big boat, they observed, and covered with a canopy of purple silk, embroidered with gold. It was rowed by twenty men, ten on each side. As it came nearer, Inga could see that in the stern, seated upon a high, cushioned chair of state, was a little man who was so very fat that he was nearly as broad as he was high. This man was dressed in a loose silken robe of purple that fell in folds to his feet, while upon his head was a cap of white velvet curiously worked with golden threads and having a circle of diamonds sewn around the band. At the opposite end of the boat stood an oddly shaped cage, and several large boxes of sandalwood were piled near the center of the craft.

As the boat approached the shore the fat little man got upon his feet and bowed several times in the direction of those who had assembled to greet him, and as he bowed he flourished his white cap in an energetic manner. His face was round as an apple and nearly as rosy. When he stopped bowing he smiled in such a sweet and happy way that Inga thought he must be a very jolly fellow.

The prow of the boat grounded on the beach, stopping its speed so suddenly that the little man was caught unawares and nearly toppled headlong into the sea. But he managed to catch hold of the chair with one hand and the hair of one of his rowers with the other, and so steadied himself. Then, again waving his jeweled cap around his head, he cried in a merry voice:

"Well, here I am at last!"

"So I perceive," responded King Kitticut, bowing with much dignity.

The fat man glanced at all the sober faces before him and burst into a rollicking laugh. Perhaps I should say it was half laughter and half a chuckle of merriment, for the sounds he emitted were quaint and droll and tempted every hearer to laugh with him.

"Heh, heh—ho, ho, ho!" he roared. "Didn't expect me, I see. Keek-eek-eek-eek! This is funny —it's really funny. Didn't know I was coming, did you? Hoo, hoo, hoo, hoo! This is certainly amusing. But I'm here, just the same."

"Hush up!" said a deep, growling voice. "You're making yourself ridiculous."

Everyone looked to see where this voice came from; but none could guess who had uttered the words of rebuke. The rowers of the boat were all solemn and silent and certainly no one on the shore had spoken. But the little man did not seem astonished in the least, or even annoyed.

King Kitticut now addressed the stranger, saying courteously:

"You are welcome to the Kingdom of Pingaree. Perhaps you will deign to come ashore and at your convenience inform us whom we have the honor of receiving as a guest."

"Thanks; I will," returned the little fat man, waddling from his place in the boat and stepping, with some difficulty, upon the sandy beach. "I am King Rinkitink, of the City of Gilgad in the Kingdom of Rinkitink, and I have come to Pingaree to see for myself the monarch who sends to my city so many beautiful pearls. I have long wished to visit this island; and so, as I said before, here I am!"

"I am pleased to welcome you," said King Kitticut. "But why has Your Majesty so few attendants? Is it not dangerous for the King of a great country to make distant journeys in one frail boat, and with but twenty men?"

"Oh, I suppose so," answered King Rinkitink, with a laugh. "But what else could I do? My subjects would not allow me to go anywhere at all, if they knew it. So I just ran away."

"Ran away!" exclaimed King Kitticut in surprise.

"Funny, isn't it? Heh, heh, heh—woo, hoo!" laughed Rinkitink, and this is as near as I can spell with letters the jolly sounds of his laughter. "Fancy a King running away from his own people—hoo, hoo—keek, eek, eek, eek! But I had to, don't you see!"

"Why?" asked the other King.

"They're afraid I'll get into mischief. They don't trust me. Keek-eek-eek—Oh, dear me! Don't trust their own King. Funny, isn't it?"

"No harm can come to you on this island," said Kitticut, pretending not to notice the odd ways of his guest. "And, whenever it pleases you to return to your own country, I will send with you a fitting escort of my own people. In the meantime, pray accompany me to my palace, where everything shall be done to make you comfortable and happy."

"Much obliged," answered Rinkitink, tipping his white cap over his left ear and heartily shaking the hand of his brother monarch. "I'm sure you can make me comfortable if you've plenty to eat. And as for being happy—ha, ha, ha, ha!— why, that's my trouble. I'm *too* happy. But stop! I've brought you some presents in those boxes. Please order your men to carry them up to the palace."

"Certainly," answered King Kitticut, well pleased, and at once he gave his men the proper orders.

"And, by the way," continued the fat little King, "let them also take my goat from his cage."

"A goat!" exclaimed the King of Pingaree.

"Exactly; my goat Bilbil. I always ride him wherever I go, for I'm not at all fond of walking, being a trifle stout—eh, Kitticut?—a trifle stout! Hoo, hoo, hoo—keek, eek!"

The Pingaree people started to lift the big cage out of the boat, but just then a gruff voice cried: "Be careful, you villains!" and as the words seemed to come from the goat's mouth the men were so astonished that they dropped the cage upon the sand with a sudden jar.

"There! I told you so!" cried the voice angrily. "You've rubbed the skin off my left knee. Why on earth didn't you handle me gently?"

"There, there, Bilbil," said King Rinkitink soothingly; "don't scold, my boy. Remember that these are strangers, and we their guests." Then he turned to Kitticut and remarked: "You have no talking goats on your island, I suppose."

"We have no goats at all," replied the King; "nor have we any animals, of any sort, who are able to talk."

"I wish my animal couldn't talk, either," said Rinkitink, winking comically at Inga and then looking toward the cage. "He is very cross at times, and indulges in language that is not respectful. I thought, at first, it would be fine to have a talking goat, with whom I could converse as I rode about my city on his back; but—keek-eek-eek-eek!—the rascal treats me as if I were a chimney sweep instead of a King. Heh, heh, heh, keek, eek! A chimney sweep—hoo, hoo, hoo!—and me a King! Funny, isn't it?" This last was addressed to Prince Inga, whom he chucked familiarly under the chin, to the boy's great embarrassment.

"Why do you not ride a horse?" asked King Kitticut.

"I can't climb upon his back, being rather stout; that's why. Kee, kee, keek, eek!—rather stout—hoo, hoo, hoo!" He paused to wipe the tears of merriment from his eyes and then added: "But I can get on and off Bilbil's back with ease."

He now opened the cage and the goat deliberately walked out and looked about him in a sulky manner. One of the rowers brought from the boat a saddle made of red velvet and beautifully embroidered with silver thistles, which he fastened upon the goat's back. The fat King put his leg over the saddle and seated himself comfortably, saying:

"Lead on, my noble host, and we will follow."

"What! Up that steep hill?" cried the goat. "Get off my back at once, Rinkitink, or I won't budge a step."

"But—consider, Bilbil," remonstrated the King. "How am I to get up that hill unless I ride?"

"Walk!" growled Bilbil.

"But I'm too fat. Really, Bilbil, I'm surprised at you. Haven't I brought you all this distance so you may see something of the world and enjoy life? And now you are so ungrateful as to refuse to carry me! Turn about is fair play, my boy. The boat carried you to this shore, because you can't swim, and now you must carry me up the hill, because I can't climb. Eh, Bilbil, isn't that reasonable?"

"Well, well, well," said the goat, surlily, "keep quiet and I'll carry you. But you make me very tired, Rinkitink, with your ceaseless chatter."

After making this protest Bilbil began walking up the hill, carrying the fat King upon his back with no difficulty whatever.

Prince Inga and his father and all the men of Pingaree were much astonished to overhear this dispute between King Rinkitink and his goat; but they were too polite to make critical remarks in the presence of their guests. King Kitticut walked beside the goat and the Prince followed after, the men coming last with the boxes of sandalwood.

When they neared the palace, the Queen and her maidens came out to meet them and the royal guest was escorted in state to the splendid throne room of the palace. Here the boxes were opened and King Rinkitink displayed all the beautiful silks and laces and jewelry with which they were filled. Every one of the courtiers and ladies received a handsome present, and the King and Queen had many rich gifts and Inga not a few. Thus the time passed pleasantly until the Chamberlain announced that dinner was served.

Bilbil the goat declared that he preferred eating of the sweet, rich grass that grew abundantly

in the palace grounds, and Rinkitink said that the beast could never bear being shut up in a stable; so they removed the saddle from his back and allowed him to wander wherever he pleased.

During the dinner Inga divided his attention between admiring the pretty gifts he had received and listening to the jolly sayings of the fat King, who laughed when he was not eating and ate when he was not laughing and seemed to enjoy himself immensely.

"For four days I have lived in that narrow boat," said he, "with no other amusement than to watch the rowers and quarrel with Bilbil; so I am very glad to be on land again with such friendly and agreeable people."

"You do us great honor," said King Kitticut, with a polite bow.

"Not at all—not at all, my brother. This Pingaree must be a wonderful island, for its pearls are the admiration of all the world; nor will I deny the fact that my kingdom would be a poor one without the riches and glory it derives from the trade in your pearls. So I have wished for many years to come here to see you, but my people said: 'No! Stay at home and behave yourself, or we'll know the reason why.'"

"Will they not miss Your Majesty from your palace at Gilgad?" inquired Kitticut.

"I think not," answered Rinkitink. "You see, one of my clever subjects has written a parchment entitled 'How to be Good,' and I believed it would benefit me to study it, as I consider the accomplishment of being good one of the fine arts. I had just scolded severely my Lord High Chancellor for coming to breakfast without combing his eyebrows, and was so sad and regretful at having hurt the poor man's feelings that I decided to shut myself up in my own room and study the scroll until I knew how to be good—hee, heek, keek, eek, eek!—to be good! Clever idea, that, wasn't it? Mighty clever! And I issued a decree that no one should enter my room, under pain of my royal displeasure, until I was ready to come out. They're awfully afraid of my royal displeasure, although not a bit afraid of me. Then I put the parchment in my pocket and escaped through the back door to my boat—and here I am. Oo, hoo-hoo, keek-eek! Imagine the fuss there would be in Gilgad if my subjects knew where I am this very minute!"

"I would like to see that parchment," said the solemn-eyed Prince Inga, "for if it indeed teaches one to be good it must be worth its weight in pearls."

"Oh, it's a fine essay," said Rinkitink, "and beautifully written with a goosequill. Listen to this: You'll enjoy it—tee, hee, hee!—enjoy it."

He took from his pocket a scroll of parchment tied with a black ribbon, and having carefully unrolled it, he proceeded to read as follows:

" 'A Good Man is One who is Never Bad.' How's that, eh? Fine thought, what? 'Therefore, in order to be Good, you must avoid those Things which are Evil.' Oh, hoo-hoo-hoo!—how clever! When I get back I shall make the man who wrote that a royal hippolorum, for, beyond question, he is the wisest man in my kingdom —as he has often told me himself." With this, Rinkitink lay back in his chair and chuckled his queer chuckle until he coughed, and coughed until he choked and choked until he sneezed. And he wrinkled his face in such a jolly, droll way that few could keep from laughing with him, and even the good Queen was forced to titter behind her fan.

When Rinkitink had recovered from his fit of laughter and had wiped his eyes upon a fine lace handkerchief, Prince Inga said to him:

"The parchment speaks truly."

"Yes, it is true beyond doubt," answered Rinkitink, "and if I could persuade Bilbil to read it he would be a much better goat than he is now. Here is another selection: 'To avoid saying Unpleasant Things, always Speak Agreeably.' That would hit Bilbil, to a dot. And here is one that applies to you, my Prince: 'Good Children are seldom punished, for the reason that they deserve no punishment.' Now, I think that is neatly put, and shows the author to be a deep thinker. But the advice that has impressed me the most is in the following paragraph: 'You may not find it as Pleasant to be Good as it is to be Bad, but Other People will find it more Pleasant.' Haw-hoo-ho! keek-eek! 'Other people will find it more pleasant!'—hee, hee, heek, keek! —'more pleasant.' Dear me—dear me! Therein lies a noble incentive to be good, and whenever I get time I'm surely going to try it."

Then he wiped his eyes again with the lace handkerchief and, suddenly remembering his dinner, seized his knife and fork and began eating.

The Warriors from the North

CHAPTER 3

KING Rinkitink was so much pleased with the Island of Pingaree that he continued his stay day after day and week after week, eating good dinners, talking with King Kitticut and sleeping. Once in a while he would read from his scroll. "For," said he, "whenever I return home, my subjects will be anxious to know if I have learned 'How to be Good,' and I must not disappoint them."

The twenty rowers lived on the small end of the island, with the pearl fishers, and seemed not to care whether they ever returned to the Kingdom of Rinkitink or not. Bilbil the goat wandered over the grassy slopes, or among the trees, and passed his days exactly as he pleased.

His master seldom cared to ride him. Bilbil was a rare curiosity to the islanders, but since there was little pleasure in talking with the goat they kept away from him. This pleased the creature, who seemed well satisfied to be left to his own devices.

Once Prince Inga, wishing to be courteous, walked up to the goat and said: "Good morning, Bilbil."

"It isn't a good morning," answered Bilbil grumpily. "It is cloudy and damp, and looks like rain."

"I hope you are contented in our kingdom," continued the boy, politely ignoring the other's harsh words.

"I'm not," said Bilbil. "I'm never contented; so it doesn't matter to me whether I'm in your kingdom or in some other kingdom. Go away—will you?"

"Certainly," answered the Prince, and after this rebuff he did not again try to make friends with Bilbil.

Now that the King, his father, was so much occupied with his royal guest, Inga was often left to amuse himself, for a boy could not be allowed to take part in the conversation of two great monarchs. He devoted himself to his studies, therefore, and day after day he climbed into the branches of his favorite tree and sat for hours in his "tree-top rest," reading his father's precious manuscripts and thinking upon what he read.

You must not think that Inga was a molly-coddle or a prig, because he was so solemn and studious. Being a King's son and heir to a throne, he could not play with the other boys of Pingaree, and he lived so much in the society of the King and Queen, and was so surrounded by the pomp and dignity of a court, that he missed all the jolly times that boys usually have. I have no doubt that had he been able to live as other boys do, he would have been much like other boys; as it was, he was subdued by his surroundings, and more grave and thoughtful than one of his years should be.

Inga was in his tree one morning when, without warning, a great fog enveloped the Island of Pingaree. The boy could scarcely see the tree next to that in which he sat, but the leaves above him prevented the dampness from wetting him, so he curled himself up in his seat and fell fast asleep.

All that forenoon the fog continued. King Kitticut, who sat in his palace talking with his merry visitor, ordered the candles lighted, that they might be able to see one another. The good Queen, Inga's mother, found it was too dark to work at her embroidery, so she called her maidens together and told them wonderful stories of

King Bertram with stern, steadfast eye

bygone days, in order to pass away the dreary hours.

But soon after noon the weather changed. The dense fog rolled away like a heavy cloud and suddenly the sun shot his bright rays over the island.

"Very good!" exclaimed King Kitticut. "We shall have a pleasant afternoon, I am sure," and he blew out the candles.

Then he stood a moment motionless, as if turned to stone, for a terrible cry from without the palace reached his ears—a cry so full of fear and horror that the King's heart almost stopped beating. Immediately there was a scurrying of feet as every one in the palace, filled with dismay, rushed outside to see what had happened. Even fat little Rinkitink sprang from his chair and followed his host and the others through the arched vestibule.

After many years the worst fears of King Kitticut were realized.

Landing upon the beach, which was but a few steps from the palace itself, were hundreds of boats, every one filled with a throng of fierce warriors. They sprang upon the land with wild shouts of defiance and rushed to the King's palace, waving aloft their swords and spears and battle-axes.

King Kitticut, so completely surprised that he

was bewildered, gazed at the approaching host with terror and grief.

"They are the men of Regos and Coregos!" he groaned. "We are, indeed, lost!"

Then he bethought himself, for the first time, of his wonderful pearls. Turning quickly, he ran back into the palace and hastened to the hall where the treasures were hidden. But the leader of the warriors had seen the King enter the palace and bounded after him, thinking he meant to escape. Just as the King had stooped to press the secret spring in the tiles, the warrior seized him from the rear and threw him backward upon the floor, at the same time shouting to his men to fetch ropes and bind the prisoner. This they did very quickly and King Kitticut soon found himself helplessly bound and in the power of his enemies. In this sad condition he was lifted by the warriors and carried outside, when the good King looked upon a sorry sight.

The Queen and her maidens, the officers and servants of the royal household and all who had inhabited this end of the Island of Pingaree had been seized by the invaders and bound with ropes. At once they began carrying their victims to the boats, tossing them in as unceremoniously as if they had been bales of merchandise.

The King looked around for his son Inga, but failed to find the boy among the prisoners. Nor

was the fat King, Rinkitink, to be seen anywhere about.

The warriors were swarming over the palace
like bees in a hive, seeking anyone who might
be in hiding, and after the search had been pro-
longed for some time the leader asked impa-
tiently: "Do you find anyone else?"

"No," his men told him. "We have captured
them all."

"Then," commanded the leader, "remove
everything of value from the palace and tear
down its walls and towers, so that not one stone
remains upon another!"

While the warriors were busy with this task
we will return to the boy Prince, who, when the
fog lifted and the sun came out, wakened from
his sleep and began to climb down from his
perch in the tree. But the terrifying cries of the
people, mingled with the shouts of the rude warriors, caused him to pause and listen eagerly.

Then he climbed rapidly up the tree, far above
his platform, to the topmost swaying branches.
This tree, which Inga called his own, was somewhat taller than the other trees that surrounded
it, and when he had reached the top he pressed
aside the leaves and saw a great fleet of boats
upon the shore—strange boats, with banners
that he had never seen before. Turning to look
upon his father's palace, he found it surrounded
by a horde of enemies. Then Inga knew the

truth: that the island had been invaded by the barbaric warriors from the north. He grew so faint from the terror of it all that he might have fallen had he not wound his arms around a limb and clung fast until the dizzy feeling passed away. Then with his sash he bound himself to the limb and again ventured to look out through the leaves.

The warriors were now engaged in carrying King Kitticut and Queen Garee and all their other captives down to the boats, where they were thrown in and chained one to another. It was a dreadful sight for the Prince to witness, but he sat very still, concealed from the sight of anyone below by the bower of leafy branches around him. Inga knew very well that he could do nothing to help his beloved parents, and that if he came down he would only be forced to share their cruel fate.

Now a procession of the Northmen passed between the boats and the palace, bearing the rich furniture, splendid draperies and rare ornaments of which the royal palace had been robbed, together with such food and other plunder as they could lay their hands upon. After this, the men of Regos and Coregos threw ropes around the marble domes and towers and hundreds of warriors tugged at these ropes until the domes and towers toppled and fell in ruins upon the ground. Then the walls themselves were torn

down, till little remained of the beautiful palace but a vast heap of white marble blocks tumbled and scattered upon the ground.

Prince Inga wept bitter tears of grief as he watched the ruin of his home; yet he was powerless to avert the destruction. When the palace had been demolished, some of the warriors entered their boats and rowed along the coast of the island, while the others marched in a great body down the length of the island itself. They were so numerous that they formed a line stretching from shore to shore and they destroyed every house they came to and took every inhabitant prisoner.

The pearl fishers who lived at the lower end of the island tried to escape in their boats, but they were soon overtaken and made prisoners, like the others. Nor was there any attempt to resist the foe, for the sharp spears and pikes and swords of the invaders terrified the hearts of the defenseless people of Pingaree, whose sole weapons were their oyster rakes.

When night fell the whole of the Island of Pingaree had been conquered by the men of the North, and all its people were slaves of the conquerors. Next morning the men of Regos and Coregos, being capable of no further mischief, departed from the scene of their triumph, carrying their prisoners with them and taking also every boat to be found upon the island. Many

of the boats they had filled with rich plunder,
with pearls and silks and velvets, with silver and
gold ornaments and all the treasure that had
made Pingaree famed as one of the richest king-
doms in the world. And the hundreds of slaves
they had captured would be set to work in the
mines of Regos and the grain fields of Coregos.

So complete was the victory of the Northmen
that it is no wonder the warriors sang songs of
triumph as they hastened back to their homes.
Great rewards were awaiting them when they
showed the haughty King of Regos and the terrible Queen of Coregos the results of their ocean
raid and conquest.

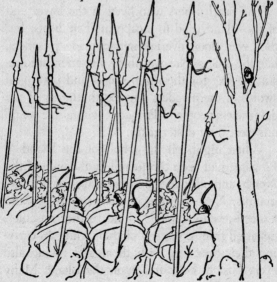

The Deserted Island

CHAPTER 4

ALL through that ter-
rible night Prince Inga
remained hidden in his
tree. In the morning he
watched the great fleet
of boats depart for their own country, carrying
his parents and his countrymen with them, as
well as everything of value the Island of Pingaree had contained.

Sad, indeed, were the boy's thoughts when
the last of the boats had become a mere speck
in the distance, but Inga did not dare leave his
perch of safety until all of the craft of the invaders had disappeared beyond the horizon.
Then he came down, very slowly and carefully,
for he was weak from hunger and the long and
weary watch, as he had been in the tree for
twenty-four hours without food.

The sun shone upon the beautiful green isle as brilliantly as if no ruthless invader had passed and laid it in ruins. The birds still chirped among the trees and the butterflies darted from flower to flower as happily as when the land was filled with a prosperous and contented people.

Inga feared that only he was left of all his nation. Perhaps he might be obliged to pass his life there alone. He would not starve, for the sea would give him oysters and fish, and the trees fruit; yet the life that confronted him was far from enticing.

The boy's first act was to walk over to where the palace had stood and search the ruins until he found some scraps of food that had been overlooked by the enemy. He sat upon a block of marble and ate of this, and tears filled his eyes as he gazed upon the desolation around him. But Inga tried to bear up bravely, and having satisfied his hunger he walked over to the well, intending to draw a bucket of drinking water.

Fortunately, this well had been overlooked by the invaders and the bucket was still fastened to the chain that wound around a stout wooden windlass. Inga took hold of the crank and began letting the bucket down into the well, when suddenly he was startled by a muffled voice crying out:

"Be careful, up there!"

The sound and the words seemed to indicate that the voice came from the bottom of the well, so Inga looked down. Nothing could be seen, on account of the darkness.

"Who are you?" he shouted.

"It's I—Rinkitink," came the answer, and the depths of the well echoed: "Tink-i-tink-i-tink!" in a ghostly manner.

"Are you in the well?" asked the boy, greatly surprised.

"Yes, and nearly drowned. I fell in while running from those terrible warriors, and I've been standing in this damp hole ever since, with my head just above the water. It's lucky the well was no deeper, for had my head been under water, instead of above it—hoo, hoo, hoo, keek, eek!—under instead of over, you know—why, then I wouldn't be talking to you now! Ha, hoo, hee!" And the well dismally echoed: "Ha, hoo, hee!" which you must imagine was a laugh half merry and half sad.

"I'm awfully sorry," cried the boy, in answer. "I wonder you have the heart to laugh at all. But how am I to get you out?"

"I've been considering that all night," said Rinkitink, "and I believe the best plan will be for you to let down the bucket to me, and I'll hold fast to it while you wind up the chain and so draw me to the top."

"I will try to do that," replied Inga, and he

let the bucket down very carefully until he heard the King call out:

"I've got it! Now pull me up—slowly, my boy, slowly—so I won't rub against the rough sides."

Inga began winding up the chain, but King Rinkitink was so fat that he was very heavy and by the time the boy had managed to pull him halfway up the well his strength was gone. He clung to the crank as long as possible, but suddenly it slipped from his grasp and the next minute he heard Rinkitink fall "plump!" into the water again.

"That's too bad!" called Inga, in real distress; "but you were so heavy I couldn't help it."

"Dear me!" gasped the King, from the darkness below, as he spluttered and coughed to get the water out of his mouth. "Why didn't you tell me you were going to let go?"

"I hadn't time," said Inga, sorrowfully.

"Well, I'm not suffering from thirst," declared the King, "for there's enough water inside me to float all the boats of Regos and Coregos— or at least it feels that way. But never mind! So long as I'm not actually drowned, what does it matter?"

"What shall we do next?" asked the boy anxiously.

"Call someone to help you," was the reply.

"There is no one on the island but myself,"

said the boy; "—excepting you," he added, as an afterthought.

"I'm not on it—more's the pity!—but *in* it," responded Rinkitink. "Are the warriors all gone?"

"Yes," said Inga, "and they have taken my father and mother, and all our people, to be their slaves," he added, trying in vain to repress a sob.

"So—so!" said Rinkitink softly; and then he paused a moment, as if in thought. Finally he said: "There are worse things than slavery, but I never imagined a well could be one of them. Tell me, Inga, could you let down some food to me? I'm nearly starved, and if you could manage to send me down some food I'd be *well* fed—hoo, hoo, heek, keek, eek!—well fed. Do you see the joke, Inga?"

"Do not ask me to enjoy a joke just now, Your Majesty," begged Inga in a sad voice; "but if you will be patient I will try to find something for you to eat."

He ran back to the ruins of the palace and began searching for bits of food with which to satisfy the hunger of the King, when to his surprise he observed the goat, Bilbil, wandering among the marble blocks.

"What!" cried Inga. "Didn't the warriors get you, either?"

"If they had," calmly replied Bilbil, "I shouldn't be here."

"But how did you escape?" asked the boy.

"Easily enough. I kept my mouth shut and stayed away from the rascals," said the goat. "I knew that the soldiers would not care for a skinny old beast like me, for to the eye of a stranger I seem good for nothing. Had they known I could talk, and that my head contained more wisdom than a hundred of their own noddles, I might not have escaped so easily."

"Perhaps you are right," said the boy.

"I suppose they got the old man?" carelessly remarked Bilbil.

"What old man?"

"Rinkitink."

"Oh, no! His Majesty is at the bottom of the well," said Inga, "and I don't know how to get him out again."

"Then let him stay there," suggested the goat.

"That would be cruel. I am sure, Bilbil, that you are fond of the good King, your master, and do not mean what you say. Together, let us find some way to save poor King Rinkitink. He is a very jolly companion, and has a heart exceedingly kind and gentle."

"Oh, well; the old boy isn't so bad, taken altogether," admitted Bilbil, speaking in a more friendly tone. "But his bad jokes and fat laughter tire me dreadfully, at times."

Prince Inga now ran back to the well, the goat following more leisurely.

"Here's Bilbil!" shouted the boy to the King. "The enemy didn't get him, it seems."

"That's lucky for the enemy," said Rinkitink. "But it's lucky for me, too, for perhaps the beast can assist me out of this hole. If you can let a rope down the well, I am sure that you and Bilbil, pulling together, will be able to drag me to the earth's surface."

"Be patient and we will make the attempt," replied Inga encouragingly, and he ran to search the ruins for a rope. Presently he found one that had been used by the warriors in toppling over the towers, which in their haste they had neglected to remove, and with some difficulty he untied the knots and carried the rope to the mouth of the well.

Bilbil had lain down to sleep and the refrain of a merry song came in muffled tones from the well, proving that Rinkitink was making a patient endeavor to amuse himself.

"I've found a rope!" Inga called down to him; and then the boy proceeded to make a loop in one end of the rope, for the King to put his arms through, and the other end he placed over the drum of the windlass. He now aroused Bilbil and fastened the rope firmly around the goat's shoulders.

"Are you ready?" asked the boy, leaning over the well.

"I am," replied the King.

"And I am not," growled the goat, "for I have not yet had my nap out. Old Rinki will be safe enough in the well until I've slept an hour or two longer."

"But it is damp in the well," protested the boy, "and King Rinkitink may catch the rheumatism, so that he will have to ride upon your back wherever he goes."

Hearing this, Bilbil jumped up at once.

"Let's get him out," he said earnestly.

"Hold fast!" shouted Inga to the King. Then he seized the rope and helped Bilbil to pull. They soon found the task more difficult than they had supposed. Once or twice the King's weight threatened to drag both the boy and the goat into the well, to keep Rinkitink company. But they pulled sturdily, being aware of this danger, and at last the King popped out of the hole and fell sprawling full length upon the ground.

For a time he lay panting and breathing hard to get his breath back, while Inga and Bilbil were likewise worn out from their long strain at the rope; so the three rested quietly upon the grass and looked at one another in silence.

Finally Bilbil said to the King: "I'm surprised at you. Why were you so foolish as to fall down that well? Don't you know it's a dangerous thing to do? You might have broken your neck in the fall, or been drowned in the water."

44

"Bilbil," replied the King solemnly, "you're a goat. Do you imagine I fell down the well on purpose?"

"I imagine nothing," retorted Bilbil. "I only know you were there."

"There? Heh-heh-heek-keek-eek! To be sure I was there," laughed Rinkitink. "There in a dark hole, where there was no light; there in a watery well, where the wetness soaked me through and through—keek-eek-eek-eek!—through and through!"

"How did it happen?" inquired Inga.

"I was running away from the enemy," explained the King, "and I was carelessly looking over my shoulder at the same time, to see if they were chasing me. So I did not see the well, but stepped into it and found myself tumbling down to the bottom. I struck the water very neatly and began struggling to keep myself from drowning, but presently I found that when I stood upon my feet on the bottom of the well, that my chin was just above the water. So I stood still and yelled for help; but no one heard me."

"If the warriors had heard you," said Bilbil, "they would have pulled you out and carried you away to be a slave. Then you would have been obliged to work for a living, and that would be a new experience."

"Work!" exclaimed Rinkitink. "Me work?

Hoo, hoo, heek-keek-eek! How absurd! I'm so stout—not to say chubby—not to say fat—that I can hardly walk, and I couldn't earn my salt at hard work. So I'm glad the enemy did not find me, Bilbil. How many others escaped?"

"That I do not know," replied the boy, "for I have not yet had time to visit the other parts of the island. When you have rested and satisfied your royal hunger, it might be well for us to look around and see what the thieving warriors of Regos and Coregos have left us."

"An excellent idea," declared Rinkitink. "I am somewhat feeble from my long confinement in the well, but I can ride upon Bilbil's back and we may as well start at once."

Hearing this, Bilbil cast a surly glance at his master but said nothing, since it was really the goat's business to carry King Rinkitink wherever he desired to go.

They first searched the ruins of the palace, and where the kitchen had once been they found a small quantity of food that had been half hidden by a block of marble. This they carefully placed in a sack to preserve it for future use, the little fat King having first eaten as much as he cared for. This consumed some time, for Rinkitink had been exceedingly hungry and liked to eat in a leisurely manner. When he had finished the meal he straddled Bilbil's back and set out

to explore the island, Prince Inga walking by his side.

They found on every hand ruin and desolation. The houses of the people had been pilfered of all valuables and then torn down or burned. Not a boat had been left upon the shore, nor was there a single person, man or woman or child, remaining upon the island, save themselves. The only inhabitants of Pingaree now consisted of a fat little King, a boy and a goat.

Even Rinkitink, merry hearted as he was, found it hard to laugh in the face of this mighty disaster. Even the goat, contrary to its usual habit, refrained from saying anything disagreeable. As for the poor boy whose home was now a wilderness, the tears came often to his eyes as he marked the ruin of his dearly loved island.

When, at nightfall, they reached the lower end of Pingaree and found it swept as bare as the rest, Inga's grief was almost more than he could bear. Everything had been swept from him—parents, home and country—in so brief a time that his bewilderment was equal to his sorrow.

Since no house remained standing, in which they might sleep, the three wanderers crept beneath the overhanging branches of a cassa tree and curled themselves up as comfortably as possible. So tired and exhausted were they by the day's anxieties and griefs that their troubles soon faded into the mists of dreamland. Beast and King and boy slumbered peacefully together until wakened by the singing of the birds which greeted the dawn of a new day.

The Three Pearls

CHAPTER 5

WHEN King Rinkitink and Prince Inga had bathed themselves in the sea and eaten a simple breakfast, they began wondering what they could do to improve their condition.

"The poor people of Gilgad," said Rinkitink cheerfully, "are little likely ever again to behold their King in the flesh, for my boat and my rowers are gone with everything else. Let us face the fact that we are imprisoned for life upon this island, and that our lives will be short unless we can secure more to eat than is in this small sack."

"I'll not starve, for I can eat grass," remarked the goat in a pleasant tone—or a tone as pleasant as Bilbil could assume.

"True, quite true," said the King. Then he seemed thoughtful for a moment and turning to Inga he asked: "Do you think, Prince, that if the worst comes, we could eat Bilbil?"

The goat gave a groan and cast a reproachful look at his master as he said:

"Monster! Would you, indeed, eat your old friend and servant?"

"Not if I can help it, Bilbil," answered the King pleasantly. "You would make a remarkably tough morsel, and my teeth are not as good as they once were."

While this talk was in progress Inga suddenly remembered the three pearls which his father had hidden under the tiled floor of the banquet hall. Without doubt King Kitticut had been so suddenly surprised by the invaders that he had found no opportunity to get the pearls, for otherwise the fierce warriors would have been defeated and driven out of Pingaree. So they must still be in their hiding place, and Inga believed they would prove of great assistance to him and his comrades in this hour of need. But the palace was a mass of ruins; perhaps he would be unable now to find the place where the pearls were hidden.

He said nothing of this to Rinkitink, remembering that his father had charged him to preserve the secret of the pearls and of their magic powers. Nevertheless, the thought of securing the wonderful treasures of his ancestors gave the boy new hope.

He stood up and said to the King:

"Let us return to the other end of Pingaree. It is more pleasant than here in spite of the desolation of my father's palace. And there, if anywhere, we shall discover a way out of our difficulties."

This suggestion met with Rinkitink's approval and the little party at once started upon the return journey. As there was no occasion to delay upon the way, they reached the big end of the island about the middle of the day and at once began searching the ruins of the palace.

They found, to their satisfaction, that one room at the bottom of a tower was still habitable, although the roof was broken in and the place was somewhat littered with stones. The King was, as he said, too fat to do any hard work, so he sat down on a block of marble and watched Inga clear the room of its rubbish. This done, the boy hunted through the ruins until he discovered a stool and an armchair that had not been broken beyond use. Some bedding and a mattress were also found, so that by nightfall the little room had been made quite comfortable.

The following morning, while Rinkitink was still sound asleep and Bilbil was busily cropping the dewy grass that edged the shore, Prince Inga began to search the tumbled heaps of marble for the place where the royal banquet hall had been. After climbing over the ruins for a time he reached a flat place which he recognized, by means of the tiled flooring and the broken furniture scattered about, to be the great hall he was seeking. But in the center of the floor, directly over the spot where the pearls were hidden, lay several large and heavy blocks of marble, which had been torn from the dismantled walls.

This unfortunate discovery for a time discouraged the boy, who realized how helpless he was to remove such vast obstacles; but it was so important to secure the pearls that he dared not give way to despair until every human effort had been made, so he sat him down to think over the matter with great care.

Meantime Rinkitink had risen from his bed and walked out upon the lawn, where he found Bilbil reclining at ease upon the greensward.

"Where is Inga?" asked Rinkitink, rubbing his eyes with his knuckles because their vision was blurred with too much sleep.

"Don't ask me," said the goat, chewing with much satisfaction a cud of sweet grasses.

"Bilbil," said the King, squatting down beside the goat and resting his fat chin upon his hands and his elbows on his knees, "allow me to confide to you the fact that I am bored, and need amusement. My good friend Kitticut has been kidnapped by the barbarians and taken from me, so there is no one to converse with me intelligently. I am the King and you are the goat. Suppose you tell me a story."

"Suppose I don't," said Bilbil, with a scowl, for a goat's face is very expressive.

"If you refuse, I shall be more unhappy than ever, and I know your disposition is too sweet to permit that. Tell me a story, Bilbil."

The goat looked at him with an expression of scorn. Said he:

"One would think you are but four years old, Rinkitink! But there—I will do as you command. Listen carefully, and the story may do you some good—although I doubt if you understand the moral."

"I am sure the story will do me good," declared the King, whose eyes were twinkling.

"Once on a time," began the goat.

"When was that, Bilbil?" asked the King gently.

"Don't interrupt; it is impolite. Once on a time there was a King with a hollow inside his head, where most people have their brains, and—"

"Is this a true story, Bilbil?"

"And the King with a hollow head could chatter words, which had no sense, and laugh in a brainless manner at senseless things. That part of the story is true enough, Rinkitink."

"Then proceed with the tale, sweet Bilbil. Yet it is hard to believe that any King could be brainless—unless, indeed, he proved it by owning a talking goat."

Bilbil glared at him a full minute in silence. Then he resumed his story:

"This empty-headed man was a King by accident, having been born to that high station. Also the King was empty-headed by the same chance, being born without brains."

"Poor fellow!" quoth the King. "Did he own a talking goat?"

"He did," answered Bilbil.

"Then he was wrong to have been born at all. Cheek-eek-eek-eek, oo, hoo!" chuckled Rinkitink, his fat body shaking with merriment. "But it's hard to prevent oneself from being born; there's no chance for protest, eh, Bilbil?"

"Who is telling this story, I'd like to know," demanded the goat, with anger.

"Ask someone with brains, my boy; I'm sure I can't tell," replied the King, bursting into one of his merry fits of laughter.

Bilbil rose to his hoofs and walked away in a dignified manner, leaving Rinkitink chuckling anew at the sour expression of the animal's face.

"Oh, Bilbil, you'll be the death of me, some day—I'm sure you will!" gasped the King, taking out his lace handkerchief to wipe his eyes; for, as he often did, he had laughed till the tears came.

Bilbil was deeply vexed and would not even turn his head to look at his master. To escape from Rinkitink he wandered among the ruins of the palace, where he came upon Prince Inga.

"Good morning, Bilbil," said the boy. "I was just going to find you, that I might consult you upon an important matter. If you will kindly turn back with me I am sure your good judgment will be of great assistance."

The angry goat was quite mollified by the respectful tone in which he was addressed, but he immediately asked:

"Are you also going to consult that empty-headed King over yonder?"

"I am sorry to hear you speak of your kind master in such a way," said the boy gravely. "All men are deserving of respect, being the highest of living creatures, and Kings deserve respect more than others, for they are set to rule over many people."

"Nevertheless," said Bilbil with conviction, "Rinkitink's head is certainly empty of brains."

"That I am unwilling to believe," insisted Inga. "But anyway his heart is kind and gentle and that is better than being wise. He is merry in spite of misfortunes that would cause others to weep and he never speaks harsh words that wound the feelings of his friends."

"Still," growled Bilbil, "he is—"

"Let us forget everything but his good nature,

which puts new heart into us when we are sad," advised the boy.

"But he is—"

"Come with me, please," interrupted Inga, "for the matter of which I wish to speak is very important."

Bilbil followed him, although the boy still heard the goat muttering that the King had no brains. Rinkitink, seeing them turn into the ruins, also followed, and upon joining them asked for his breakfast.

Inga opened the sack of food and while he and the King ate of it the boy said:

"If I could find a way to remove some of the blocks of marble which have fallen in the banquet hall, I think I could find means for us to escape from this barren island."

"Then," mumbled Rinkitink, with his mouth full, "let us move the blocks of marble."

"But how?" inquired Prince Inga. "They are very heavy."

"Ah, how, indeed?" returned the King, smacking his lips contentedly. "That is a serious question. But—I have it! Let us see what my famous parchment says about it." He wiped his fingers upon a napkin and then, taking the scroll from a pocket inside his embroidered blouse, he unrolled it and read the following words: " 'Never step on another man's toes.' "

The goat gave a snort of contempt; Inga was

silent; the King looked from one to the other inquiringly.

"That's the idea, exactly!" declared Rinkitink.

"To be sure," said Bilbil scornfully, "it tells us exactly how to move the blocks of marble."

"Oh, does it?" responded the King, and then for a moment he rubbed the top of his bald head in a perplexed manner. The next moment he burst into a peal of joyous laughter. The goat looked at Inga and sighed.

"What did I tell you?" asked the creature. "Was I right, or was I wrong?"

"This scroll," said Rinkitink, "is indeed a masterpiece. Its advice is of tremendous value. 'Never step on another man's toes.' Let us think this over. The inference is that we should step upon our own toes, which were given us for that purpose. Therefore, if I stepped upon another man's toes, I would be the other man. Hoo, hoo, hoo!—the other man—hee, hee, heek-keek-eek! Funny, isn't it?"

"Didn't I say—" began Bilbil.

"No matter what you said, my boy," roared the King. "No fool could have figured that out as nicely as I did."

"We have still to decide how to remove the blocks of marble," suggested Inga anxiously.

"Fasten a rope to them, and pull," said Bilbil. "Don't pay any more attention to Rinkitink, for he is no wiser than the man who wrote that brainless scroll. Just get the rope, and we'll fasten Rinkitink to one end of it for a weight and I'll help you pull."

"Thank you, Bilbil," replied the boy. "I'll get the rope at once."

Bilbil found it difficult to climb over the ruins to the floor of the banquet hall, but there are few places a goat cannot get to when it makes the attempt, so Bilbil succeeded at last, and even fat little Rinkitink finally joined them, though much out of breath.

Inga fastened one end of the rope around a block of marble and then made a loop at the other end to go over Bilbil's head. When all was ready the boy seized the rope and helped the goat to pull; yet, strain as they might, the huge block would not stir from its place. Seeing this,

King Rinkitink came forward and lent his assistance, the weight of his body forcing the heavy marble to slide several feet from where it had lain.

But it was hard work and all were obliged to take a long rest before undertaking the removal of the next block.

"Admit, Bilbil," said the King, "that I am of some use in the world."

"Your weight was of considerable help," acknowledged the goat, "but if your head were as well filled as your stomach the task would be still easier."

When Inga went to fasten the rope a second time he was rejoiced to discover that by moving one more block of marble he could uncover the tile with the secret spring. So the three pulled

with renewed energy and to their joy the block moved and rolled upon its side, leaving Inga free to remove the treasure when he pleased.

But the boy had no intention of allowing Bilbil and the King to share the secret of the royal treasures of Pingaree; so, although both the goat and its master demanded to know why the marble blocks had been moved, and how it would benefit them, Inga begged them to wait until the next morning, when he hoped to be able to satisfy them that their hard work had not been in vain.

Having little confidence in this promise of a mere boy, the goat grumbled and the King laughed; but Inga paid no heed to their ridicule and set himself to work rigging up a fishing rod, with line and hook. During the afternoon he waded out to some rocks near the shore and fished patiently until he had captured enough yellow perch for their supper and breakfast.

"Ah," said Rinkitink, looking at the fine catch when Inga returned to the shore; "these will taste delicious when they are cooked; but do you know how to cook them?"

"No," was the reply. I have often caught fish, but never cooked them. Perhaps Your Majesty understands cooking."

"Cooking and majesty are two different things," laughed the little King. "I could not cook a fish to save me from starvation."

"For my part," said Bilbil, "I never eat fish, but I can tell you how to cook them, for I have often watched the palace cooks at their work." And so, with the goat's assistance, the boy and the King managed to prepare the fish and cook them, after which they were eaten with good appetite.

That night, after Rinkitink and Bilbil were both fast asleep, Inga stole quietly through the moonlight to the desolate banquet hall. There, kneeling down, he touched the secret spring as his father had instructed him to do and to his joy the tile sank downward and disclosed the opening. You may imagine how the boy's heart throbbed with excitement as he slowly thrust his hand into the cavity and felt around to see if the precious pearls were still there. In a moment his fingers touched the silken bag and, without pausing to close the recess, he pressed the treasure against his breast and ran out into the moonlight to examine it. When he reached a bright place he started to open the bag, but he observed Bilbil lying asleep upon the grass near by. So, trembling with the fear of discovery, he ran to another place, and when he paused he heard Rinkitink snoring lustily. Again he fled and made his way to the seashore, where he squatted under a bank and began to untie the cords that fastened the mouth of the bag. But now another fear assailed him.

"If the pearls should slip from my hand," he thought, "and roll into the water, they might be lost to me forever. I must find some safer place."

Here and there he wandered, still clasping the silken bag in both hands, and finally he went to the grove and climbed into the tall tree where he had made his platform and seat. But here it was pitch dark, so he found he must wait patiently until morning before he dared touch the pearls. During those hours of waiting he had time for reflection and reproached himself for being so frightened by the possession of his father's treasures.

"These pearls have belonged to our family for generations," he mused, "yet no one has ever lost them. If I use ordinary care I am sure I need have no fears for their safety."

When the dawn came and he could see plainly, Inga opened the bag and took out the Blue Pearl. There was no possibility of his being observed by others, so he took time to examine it wonderingly, saying to himself: "This will give me strength."

Taking off his right shoe he placed the Blue Pearl within it, far up in the pointed toe. Then he tore a piece from his handkerchief and stuffed it into the shoe to hold the pearl in place. Inga's shoes were long and pointed, as were all the shoes worn in Pingaree, and the points curled upward, so that there was quite a vacant space beyond the place where the boy's toes reached when the shoe was upon his foot.

After he had put on the shoe and laced it up he opened the bag and took out the Pink Pearl. "This will protect me from danger," said Inga, and removing the shoe from his left foot he carefully placed the pearl in the hollow toe. This, also, he secured in place by means of a strip torn from his handkerchief.

Having put on the second shoe and laced it up, the boy drew from the silken bag the third pearl—that which was pure white—and holding it to his ear he asked:

"Will you advise me what to do, in this my hour of misfortune?"

Clearly the small voice of the pearl made answer:

"I advise you to go to the Islands of Regos and Coregos, where you may liberate your parents from slavery."

"How could I do that?" exclaimed Prince Inga, amazed at receiving such advice.

"To-night," spoke the voice of the pearl, "there will be a storm, and in the morning a boat will strand upon the shore. Take this boat and row to Regos and Coregos."

"How can I, a weak boy, pull the boat so far?" he inquired, doubting the possibility.

"The Blue Pearl will give you strength," was the reply.

"But I may be shipwrecked and drowned, before ever I reach Regos and Coregos," protested the boy.

"The Pink Pearl will protect you from harm," murmured the voice, soft and low but very distinct.

"Then I shall act as you advise me," declared Inga, speaking firmly because this promise gave him courage, and as he removed the pearl from his ear it whispered:

"The wise and fearless are sure to win success."

Restoring the White Pearl to the depths of the silken bag, Inga fastened it securely around his neck and buttoned his waist above it to hide the treasure from all prying eyes. Then he slowly climbed down from the tree and returned to the room where King Rinkitink still slept.

The goat was browsing upon the grass but looked cross and surly. When the boy said good morning as he passed, Bilbil made no response whatever. As Inga entered the room the King awoke and asked:

"What is that mysterious secret of yours? I've been dreaming about it, and I haven't got my breath yet from tugging at those heavy blocks. Tell me the secret."

"A secret told is no longer a secret," replied Inga, with a laugh. "Besides, this is a family secret, which it is proper I should keep to myself. But I may tell you one thing, at least: We are going to leave this island to-morrow morning."

The King seemed puzzled by this statement.

"I'm not much of a swimmer," said he, "and, though I'm fat enough to float upon the surface of the water, I'd only bob around and get nowhere at all."

"We shall not swim, but ride comfortably in a boat," promised Inga.

"There isn't a boat on this island!" declared Rinkitink, looking upon the boy with wonder.

"True," said Inga. "But one will come to us in the morning." He spoke positively, for he had perfect faith in the promise of the White Pearl; but Rinkitink, knowing nothing of the three marvelous jewels, began to fear that the little Prince had lost his mind through grief and misfortune.

For this reason the King did not question the boy further but tried to cheer him by telling him witty stories. He laughed at all the stories himself, in his merry, rollicking way, and Inga joined freely in the laughter because his heart had been lightened by the prospect of rescuing his dear parents. Not since the fierce warriors had descended upon Pingaree had the boy been so hopeful and happy.

With Rinkitink riding upon Bilbil's back, the three made a tour of the island and found in the central part some bushes and trees bearing ripe fruit. They gathered this freely, for—aside from the fish which Inga caught—it was the only food they now had, and the less they had, the bigger Rinkitink's appetite seemed to grow.

"I am never more happy," said he with a sigh, "than when I am eating."

Toward evening the sky became overcast and soon a great storm began to rage. Prince Inga and King Rinkitink took refuge within the shelter of the room they had fitted up and there Bilbil joined them. The goat and the King were somewhat disturbed by the violence of the storm, but Inga did not mind it, being pleased at this evidence that the White Pearl might be relied upon.

All night the wind shrieked around the island; thunder rolled, lightning flashed and rain came down in torrents. But with morning the storm abated and when the sun arose no sign of the tempest remained save a few fallen trees.

The Magic Boat

CHAPTER 6

PRINCE Inga was up
with the sun and, ac-
companied by Bilbil, be-
gan walking along the
shore in search of the
boat which the White Pearl had promised him.
Never for an instant did he doubt that he would
find it and before he had walked any great distance a dark object at the water's edge caught
his eye.

"It is the boat, Bilbil!" he cried joyfully, and
running down to it he found it was, indeed, a
large and roomy boat. Although stranded upon
the beach, it was in perfect order and had suf-
fered in no way from the storm.

Inga stood for some moments gazing upon the
handsome craft and wondering where it could

have come from. Certainly it was unlike any boat he had ever seen. On the outside it was painted a lustrous black, without any other color to relieve it; but all the inside of the boat was lined with pure silver, polished so highly that the surface resembled a mirror and glinted brilliantly in the rays of the sun. The seats had white velvet cushions upon them and the cushions were splendidly embroidered with threads of gold. At one end, beneath the broad seat, was a small barrel with silver hoops, which the boy found was filled with fresh, sweet water. A great chest of sandalwood, bound and ornamented with silver, stood in the other end of the boat. Inga raised the lid and discovered the chest filled with sea-biscuits, cakes, tinned meats and ripe, juicy melons; enough good and wholesome food to last the party a long time.

Lying upon the bottom of the boat were two shining oars, and overhead, but rolled back now, was a canopy of silver cloth to ward off the heat of the sun.

It is no wonder the boy was delighted with the appearance of this beautiful boat; but on reflection he feared it was too large for him to row any great distance. Unless, indeed, the Blue Pearl gave him unusual strength.

While he was considering this matter, King Rinkitink came waddling up to him and said:

"Well, well, well, my Prince, your words have

come true! Here is the boat, for a certainty, yet how it came here—and how you knew it would come to us—are puzzles that mystify me. I do not question our good fortune, however, and my heart is bubbling with joy, for in this boat I will return at once to my City of Gilgad, from which I have remained absent altogether too long a time."

"I do not wish to go to Gilgad," said Inga.

"That is too bad, my friend, for you would be very welcome. But you may remain upon this island, if you wish," continued Rinkitink, "and when I get home I will send some of my people to rescue you."

"It is my boat, Your Majesty," said Inga quietly.

"May be, may be," was the careless answer, "but I am King of a great country, while you are a boy Prince without any kingdom to speak of. Therefore, being of greater importance than you, it is just and right that I take your boat and return to my own country in it."

"I am sorry to differ from Your Majesty's views," said Inga, "but instead of going to Gilgad I consider it of greater importance that we go to the islands of Regos and Coregos."

"Hey? What!" cried the astounded King. "To Regos and Coregos! To become slaves of the barbarians, like the King, your father? No, no,

my boy! Your Uncle Rinki may have an empty
noddle, as Bilbil claims, but he is far too wise to
put his head in the lion's mouth. It's no fun to
be a slave."

"The people of Regos and Coregos will not
enslave us," declared Inga. "On the contrary, it
is my intention to set free my dear parents, as
well as all my people, and to bring them back
again to Pingaree."

"Cheek-eek-eek-eek-eek! How funny!" chuckled Rinkitink, winking at the goat, which
scowled in return. "Your audacity takes my
breath away, Inga, but the adventure has its
charm, I must confess. Were I not so fat, I'd
agree to your plan at once, and could probably
conquer that horde of fierce warriors without
any assistance at all—any at all—eh, Bilbil? But
I grieve to say that I am fat, and not in good
fighting trim. As for your determination to do
what I admit I can't do, Inga, I fear you forget
that you are only a boy, and rather small at
that."

"No, I do not forget that," was Inga's reply.

"Then please consider that you and I and Bilbil are not strong enough, as an army, to conquer
a powerful nation of skilled warriors. We could
attempt it, of course, but you are too young to
die, while I am too old. Come with me to my
City of Gilgad, where you will be greatly hon-

ored. I'll have my professors teach you how to
be good. Eh? What do you say?"

Inga was a little embarrassed how to reply to
these arguments, which he knew King Rinkitink considered were wise; so, after a period of
thought, he said:

"I will make a bargain with Your Majesty,
for I do not wish to fail in respect to so worthy
a man and so great a King as yourself. This boat
is mine, as I have said, and in my father's absence you have become my guest; therefore I
claim that I am entitled to some consideration,
as well as you."

"No doubt of it," agreed Rinkitink. "What is
the bargain you propose, Inga?"

"Let us both get into the boat, and you shall
first try to row us to Gilgad. If you succeed, I
will accompany you right willingly; but should
you fail, I will then row the boat to Regos, and
you must come with me without further protest."

"A fair and just bargain!" cried the King,
highly pleased. "Yet, although I am a man of
mighty deeds, I do not relish the prospect of
rowing so big a boat all the way to Gilgad. But
I will do my best and abide by the result."

The matter being thus peaceably settled, they
prepared to embark. A further supply of fruits
was placed in the boat and Inga also raked up a
quantity of the delicious oysters that abounded

on the coast of Pingaree but which he had before been unable to reach for lack of a boat. This was done at the suggestion of the ever-hungry Rinkitink, and when the oysters had been stowed in their shells behind the water barrel and a plentiful supply of grass brought aboard for Bilbil, they decided they were ready to start on their voyage.

It proved no easy task to get Bilbil into the boat, for he was a remarkably clumsy goat and once, when Rinkitink gave him a push, he tumbled into the water and nearly drowned before they could get him out again. But there was no thought of leaving the quaint animal behind. His power of speech made him seem almost human in the eyes of the boy, and the fat King was so accustomed to his surly companion that nothing could have induced him to part with him. Finally Bilbil fell sprawling into the bottom of the boat, and Inga helped him to get to the front end, where there was enough space for him to lie down.

Rinkitink now took his seat in the silver-lined craft and the boy came last, pushing off the boat as he sprang aboard, so that it floated freely upon the water.

"Well, here we go for Gilgad!" exclaimed the King, picking up the oars and placing them in the row-locks. Then he began to row as hard as

he could, singing at the same time an odd sort of
a song that ran like this:

"The way to Gilgad isn't bad
For a stout old King and a brave young lad,
For a cross old goat with a dripping coat,
And a silver boat in which to float.
So our hearts are merry, light and glad
As we speed away to fair Gilgad!"

"Don't, Rinkitink; please don't! It makes me
seasick," growled Bilbil.

Rinkitink stopped rowing, for by this time he
was all out of breath and his round face was
covered with big drops of perspiration. And
when he looked over his shoulder he found to
his dismay that the boat had scarcely moved a
foot from its former position.

Inga said nothing and appeared not to notice
the King's failure. So now Rinkitink, with a
serious look on his fat, red face, took off his
purple robe and rolled up the sleeves of his
tunic and tried again.

However, he succeeded no better than before
and when he heard Bilbil give a gruff laugh and
saw a smile upon the boy Prince's face, Rinkitink suddenly dropped the oars and began shouting with laughter at his own defeat. As he wiped
his brow with a yellow silk handkerchief he sang
in a merry voice:

"A sailor bold am I, I hold,
But boldness will not row a boat.
So I confess I'm in distress
And just as useless as the goat."

"Please leave me out of your verses," said Bilbil with a snort of anger.

"When I make a fool of myself, Bilbil, I'm a goat," replied Rinkitink.

"Not so," insisted Bilbil. "Nothing could make you a member of my superior race."

"Superior? Why, Bilbil, a goat is but a beast, while I am a King!"

"I claim that superiority lies in intelligence," said the goat.

Rinkitink paid no attention to this remark, but turning to Inga he said:

"We may as well get back to the shore, for the boat is too heavy to row to Gilgad or anywhere else. Indeed, it will be hard for us to reach land again."

"Let me take the oars," suggested Inga. "You must not forget our bargain."

"No, indeed," answered Rinkitink. "If you can row us to Regos, or to any other place, I will go with you without protest."

So the King took Inga's place in the stern of the boat and the boy grasped the oars and commenced to row. And now, to the great wonder of Rinkitink—and even to Inga's surprise—the

oars became light as feathers as soon as the Prince took hold of them. In an instant the boat began to glide rapidly through the water and, seeing this, the boy turned its prow toward the north. He did not know exactly where Regos and Coregos were located, but he did know that the islands lay to the north of Pingaree, so he decided to trust to luck and the guidance of the pearls to carry him to them.

Gradually the Island of Pingaree became smaller to their view as the boat sped onward, until at the end of an hour they had lost sight of it altogether and were wholly surrounded by the purple waters of the Nonestic Ocean.

Prince Inga did not tire from the labor of rowing; indeed, it seemed to him no labor at all.

Once he stopped long enough to place the poles of the canopy in the holes that had been made for them, in the edges of the boat, and to spread the canopy of silver over the poles, for Rinkitink had complained of the sun's heat. But the canopy shut out the hot rays and rendered the interior of the boat cool and pleasant.

"This is a glorious ride!" cried Rinkitink, as he lay back in the shade. "I find it a decided relief to be away from that dismal island of Pingaree."

"It may be a relief for a short time," said Bilbil, "but you are going to the land of your enemies, who will probably stick your fat body full of spears and arrows."

"Oh, I hope not!" exclaimed Inga, distressed at the thought.

79

"Never mind," said the King calmly, "a man can die but once, you know, and when the enemy kills me I shall beg him to kill Bilbil, also, that we may remain together in death as in life."

"They may be cannibals, in which case they will roast and eat us," suggested Bilbil, who wished to terrify his master.

"Who knows?" answered Rinkitink, with a shudder. "But cheer up, Bilbil; they may not klll us after all, or even capture us; so let us not borrow trouble. Do not look so cross, my sprightly quadruped, and I will sing to amuse you."

"Your song would make me more cross than ever," grumbled the goat.

"Quite impossible, dear Bilbil. You couldn't be more surly if you tried. So here is a famous song for you."

While the boy rowed steadily on and the boat rushed fast over the water, the jolly King, who never could be sad or serious for many minutes at a time, lay back on his embroidered cushions and sang as follows:

"A merry maiden went to sea—
    Sing too-ral-oo-ral-i-do!
She sat upon the Captain's knee
And looked around the sea to see
What she could see, but she couldn't see me—
    Sing too-ral-oo-ral-i-do!

"How do you like that, Bilbil?"

"I don't like it," complained the goat. "It reminds me of the alligator that tried to whistle."

"Did he succeed, Bilbil?" asked the King.

"He whistled as well as you sing."

"Ha, ha, ha, ha, heek, keek, eek!" chuckled the King. "He must have whistled most exquisitely, eh, my friend?"

"I am not your friend," returned the goat, wagging his ears in a surly manner.

"I am yours, however," was the King's cheery reply; "and to prove it I'll sing you another verse."

"Don't, I beg of you!"

But the King sang as follows:

"The wind blew off the maiden's shoe—
     Sing too-ral-oo-ral-i-do!
And the shoe flew high to the sky so blue
And the maiden knew 'twas a new shoe, too;
But she couldn't pursue the shoe, 'tis true—
     Sing too-ral-oo-ral-i-do!

"Isn't that sweet, my pretty goat?"

"Sweet, do you ask?" retorted Bilbil. "I consider it as sweet as candy made from mustard and vinegar."

"But not as sweet as your disposition, I admit. Ah, Bilbil, your temper would put honey itself to shame."

"Do not quarrel, I beg of you," pleaded Inga. "Are we not sad enough already?"

"But this is a jolly quarrel," said the King, "and it is the way Bilbil and I often amuse ourselves. Listen, now, to the last verse of all:

"The maid who shied her shoe now cried—
    Sing too-ral-oo-ral-i-do!
Her tears were fried for the Captain's bride
Who ate with pride her sobs, beside,
And gently sighed 'I'm satisfied'—
    Sing too-ral-oo-ral-i-do!"

"Worse and worse!" grumbled Bilbil, with much scorn. "I am glad that is the last verse, for another of the same kind might cause me to faint."

"I fear you have no ear for music," said the King.

"I have heard no music, as yet," declared the goat. "You must have a strong imagination, King Rinkitink, if you consider your songs music. Do you remember the story of the bear that hired out for a nursemaid?"

"I do not recall it just now," said Rinkitink, with a wink at Inga.

"Well, the bear tried to sing a lullaby to put the baby to sleep."

"And then?" said the King.

"The bear was highly pleased with its own voice, but the baby was nearly frightened to death."

"Heh, heh, heh, heh, whoo, hoo, hoo! You are a merry rogue, Bilbil," laughed the King; "a merry rogue in spite of your gloomy features. However, if I have not amused you, I have at least pleased myself, for I am exceedingly fond of a good song. So let us say no more about it."

All this time the boy Prince was rowing the boat. He was not in the least tired, for the oars he held seemed to move of their own accord. He paid little heed to the conversation of Rinkitink and the goat, but busied his thoughts with plans of what he should do when he reached the islands of Regos and Coregos and confronted his enemies. When the others finally became silent, Inga inquired:

"Can you fight, King Rinkitink?"

"I have never tried," was the answer. "In time of danger I have found it much easier to run away than to face the foe."

"But *could* you fight?" asked the boy.

"I might try, if there was no chance to escape by running. Have you a proper weapon for me to fight with?"

"I have no weapon at all," confessed Inga.

"Then let us use argument and persuasion instead of fighting. For instance, if we could persuade the warriors of Regos to lie down, and let me step on them, they would be crushed with ease."

Prince Inga had expected little support from the King, so he was not discouraged by this answer. After all, he reflected, a conquest by battle would be out of the question, yet the White Pearl would not have advised him to go to Regos and Coregos had the mission been a hopeless one. It seemed to him, on further reflection, that he must rely upon circumstances to determine his actions when he reached the islands of the barbarians.

By this time Inga felt perfect confidence in the Magic Pearls. It was the White Pearl that had given him the boat, and the Blue Pearl that had given him strength to row it. He believed that the Pink Pearl would protect him from any danger that might arise; so his anxiety was not for himself, but for his companions. King Rinkitink and the goat had no magic to protect them, so Inga resolved to do all in his power to keep them from harm.

For three days and three nights the boat with the silver lining sped swiftly over the ocean. On the morning of the fourth day, so quickly had they traveled, Inga saw before him the shores of the two great islands of Regos and Coregos.

"The pearls have guided me aright!" he whispered to himself. "Now, if I am wise, and cautious, and brave, I believe I shall be able to rescue my father and mother and my people."

The Twin Islands

CHAPTER 7

THE Island of Regos
was ten miles wide and
forty miles long and it
was ruled by a big and
powerful King named
Gos. Near to the shores were green and fertile
fields, but farther back from the sea were rugged
hills and mountains, so rocky that nothing
would grow there. But in these mountains were
mines of gold and silver, which the slaves of
the King were forced to work, being confined
in dark underground passages for that purpose.
In the course of time huge caverns had been
hollowed out by the slaves, in which they lived
and slept, never seeing the light of day. Cruel
overseers with whips stood over these poor people, who had been captured in many countries

by the raiding parties of King Gos, and the overseers were quite willing to lash the slaves with
their whips if they faltered a moment in their
work.

Between the green shores and the mountains
were forests of thick, tangled trees, between
which narrow paths had been cut to lead up to
the caves of the mines. It was on the level green
meadows, not far from the ocean, that the great
City of Regos had been built, wherein was located the palace of the King. This city was inhabited by thousands of the fierce warriors of
Gos, who frequently took to their boats and
spread over the sea to the neighboring islands to
conquer and pillage, as they had done at Pingaree. When they were not absent on one of
these expeditions, the City of Regos swarmed
with them and so became a dangerous place for
any peaceful person to live in, for the warriors
were as lawless as their King.

The Island of Coregos lay close beside the
Island of Regos; so close, indeed, that one might
have thrown a stone from one shore to another.
But Coregos was only half the size of Regos and
instead of being mountainous it was a rich and
pleasant country, covered with fields of grain.
The fields of Coregos furnished food for the
warriors and citizens of both countries, while the
mines of Regos made them all rich.

Coregos was ruled by Queen Cor, who was

wedded to King Gos; but so stern and cruel was the nature of this Queen that the people could not decide which of their sovereigns they dreaded most.

Queen Cor lived in her own City of Coregos, which lay on that side of her island facing Regos, and her slaves, who were mostly women, were made to plow the land and to plant and harvest the grain.

From Regos to Coregos stretched a bridge of boats, set close together, with planks laid across their edges for people to walk upon. In this way it was easy to pass from one island to the other and in times of danger the bridge could be quickly removed.

The native inhabitants of Regos and Coregos consisted of the warriors, who did nothing but fight and ravage, and the trembling servants who waited on them. King Gos and Queen Cor were at war with all the rest of the world. Other islanders hated and feared them, for their slaves were badly treated and absolutely no mercy was shown to the weak or ill.

When the boats that had gone to Pingaree returned loaded with rich plunder and a host of captives, there was much rejoicing in Regos and Coregos and the King and Queen gave a fine feast to the warriors who had accomplished so great a conquest. This feast was set for the warriors in the grounds of King Gos's palace, while with them in the great throne room all the captains and leaders of the fighting men were assembled with King Gos and Queen Cor, who had come from her island to attend the ceremony. Then all the goods that had been stolen from the King of Pingaree were divided according to rank, the King and Queen taking half, the captains a quarter, and the rest being divided amongst the warriors.

The day following the feast King Gos sent King Kitticut and all the men of Pingaree to work in his mines under the mountains, having first chained them together so they could not escape. The gentle Queen of Pingaree and all her women, together with the captured children, were given to Queen Cor, who set them to work in her grain fields.

Then the rulers and warriors of these dreadful islands thought they had done forever with Pingaree. Despoiled of all its wealth, its houses torn down, its boats captured and all its people enslaved, what likelihood was there that they might ever again hear of the desolated island? So the people of Regos and Coregos were surprised and puzzled when one morning they observed approaching their shores from the direction of the south a black boat containing a boy, a fat man and a goat. The warriors asked one another who these could be, and where they had come from? No one ever came to those islands of their own accord, that was certain.

Prince Inga guided his boat to the south end of the Island of Regos, which was the landing place nearest to the city, and when the warriors saw this action they went down to the shore to meet him, being led by a big captain named Buzzub.

"Those people surely mean us no good," said Rinkitink uneasily to the boy. "Without doubt they intend to capture us and make us their slaves."

"Do not fear, sir," answered Inga, in a calm voice. "Stay quietly in the boat with Bilbil until I have spoken with these men."

He stopped the boat a dozen feet from the shore, and standing up in his place made a grave bow to the multitude confronting him. Said the big Captain Buzzub in a gruff voice:

"Well, little one, who may you be? And how dare you come, uninvited and all alone, to the Island of Regos?"

"I am Inga, Prince of Pingaree," returned the boy, "and I have come here to free my parents and my people, whom you have wrongfully enslaved."

When they heard this bold speech a mighty laugh arose from the band of warriors, and when it had subsided the captain said:

"You love to jest, my baby Prince, and the joke is fairly good. But why did you willingly

thrust your head into the lion's mouth? When you were free, why did you not stay free? We did not know we had left a single person in Pingaree! But since you managed to escape us then, it is really kind of you to come here of your own free will, to be our slave. Who is the funny fat person with you?"

"It is His Majesty, King Rinkitink, of the great City of Gilgad. He has accompanied me to see that you render full restitution for all you have stolen from Pingaree."

"Better yet!" laughed Buzzub. "He will make a fine slave for Queen Cor, who loves to tickle fat men, and see them jump."

King Rinkitink was filled with horror when he heard this, but the Prince answered as boldly as before, saying:

"We are not to be frightened by bluster, believe me; nor are we so weak as you imagine. We have magic powers so great and terrible that no host of warriors can possibly withstand us, and therefore I call upon you to surrender your city and your island to us, before we crush you with our mighty powers."

The boy spoke very gravely and earnestly, but his words only aroused another shout of laughter. So while the men of Regos were laughing Inga drove the boat well up onto the sandy beach and leaped out. He also helped Rinkitink out, and when the goat had unaided sprung to the sands, the King got upon Bilbil's back, trembling a little internally, but striving to look as brave as possible.

There was a bunch of coarse hair between the goat's ears, and this Inga clutched firmly in his left hand. The boy knew the Pink Pearl would protect not only himself, but all whom he touched, from any harm, and as Rinkitink was astride the goat and Inga had his hand upon the animal, the three could not be injured by anything the warriors could do. But Captain Buzzub did not know this, and the little group of three seemed so weak and ridiculous that he believed their capture would be easy. So he turned to his men and with a wave of his hand said:

"Seize the intruders!"

Instantly two or three of the warriors stepped forward to obey, but to their amazement they could not reach any of the three; their hands were arrested as if by an invisible wall of iron. Without paying any attention to these attempts at capture, Inga advanced slowly and the goat kept pace with him. And when Rinkitink saw that he was safe from harm he gave one of his big, merry laughs, and it startled the warriors and made them nervous. Captain Buzzub's eyes grew big with surprise as the three steadily advanced and forced his men backward; nor was he free from terror himself at the magic that protected these strange visitors. As for the warriors, they presently became terror-stricken and fled in a panic up the slope toward the city, and Buzzub was obliged to chase after them and shout threats of punishment before he could halt them and form them into a line of battle.

All the men of Regos bore spears and bows-and-arrows, and some of the officers had swords and battle-axes; so Buzzub ordered them to stand their ground and shoot and slay the strangers as they approached. This they tried to do. Inga being in advance, the warriors sent a flight of sharp arrows straight at the boy's breast, while others cast their long spears at him.

It seemed to Rinkitink that the little Prince must surely perish as he stood facing this hail of murderous missiles; but the power of the Pink Pearl did not desert him, and when the arrows and spears had reached to within an inch of his body they bounded back again and fell harm-lessly at his feet. Nor were Rinkitink or Bilbil injured in the least, although they stood close beside Inga.

Buzzub stood for a moment looking upon the boy in silent wonder. Then, recovering himself, he shouted in a loud voice:

"Once again! All together, my men. No one shall ever defy our might and live!"

Again a flight of arrows and spears sped toward the three, and since many more of the

warriors of Regos had by this time joined their fellows, the air was for a moment darkened by the deadly shafts. But again all fell harmless before the power of the Pink Pearl, and Bilbil, who had been growing very angry at the attempts to injure him and his party, suddenly made a bolt forward, casting off Inga's hold, and butted into the line of warriors, who were standing amazed at their failure to conquer.

Taken by surprise at the goat's attack, a dozen big warriors tumbled in a heap, yelling with fear, and their comrades, not knowing what had happened but imagining that their foes were attacking them, turned about and ran to the city as hard as they could go. Bilbil, still angry, had just time to catch the big captain as he turned to follow his men, and Buzzub first sprawled headlong upon the ground, then rolled over two or three times, and finally jumped up and ran yelling after his defeated warriors. This butting on the part of the goat was very hard upon King Rinkitink, who nearly fell off Bilbil's back at the shock of encounter; but the little fat King wound his arms around the goat's neck and shut his eyes and clung on with all his might. It was not until he heard Inga say triumphantly, "We have won the fight without striking a blow!" that Rinkitink dared open his eyes again. Then he saw the warriors rushing into the City of Regos and barring the heavy gates, and he was very much relieved at the sight.

"Without striking a blow!" said Bilbil indignantly. "That is not quite true, Prince Inga. You did not fight, I admit, but I struck a couple of times to good purpose, and I claim to have conquered the cowardly warriors unaided."

"You and I together, Bilbil," said Rinkitink mildly. "But the next time you make a charge, please warn me in time, so that I may dismount and give you all the credit for the attack."

There being no one now to oppose their advance, the three walked to the gates of the city, which had been closed against them. The gates were of iron and heavily barred, and upon the top of the high walls of the city a host of the warriors now appeared armed with arrows and spears and other weapons. For Buzzub had gone straight to the palace of King Gos and reported his defeat, relating the powerful magic of the boy, the fat King and the goat, and had asked what to do next.

The big captain still trembled with fear, but King Gos did not believe in magic, and called Buzzub a coward and a weakling. At once the King took command of his men personally, and he ordered the walls manned with warriors and instructed them to shoot to kill if any of the three strangers approached the gates.

Of course, neither Rinkitink nor Bilbil knew how they had been protected from harm and so at first they were inclined to resent the boy's command that the three must always keep together and touch one another at all times. But when Inga explained that his magic would not otherwise save them from injury, they agreed to obey, for they had now seen enough to convince them that the Prince was really protected by some invisible power.

As they came before the gates another shower of arrows and spears descended upon them, and as before not a single missile touched their bodies. King Gos, who was upon the wall, was greatly amazed and somewhat worried, but he depended upon the strength of his gates and commanded his men to continue shooting until all their weapons were gone.

Inga let them shoot as much as they wished, while he stood before the great gates and examined them carefully.

"Perhaps Bilbil can batter down the gates," suggested Rinkitink.

"No," replied the goat; "my head is hard, but not harder than iron."

"Then," returned the King, "let us stay outside; especially as we can't get in."

But Inga was not at all sure they could not get in. The gates opened inward, and three heavy bars were held in place by means of stout staples riveted to the sheets of steel. The boy had been told that the power of the Blue Pearl would enable him to accomplish any feat of strength, and he believed that this was true.

The warriors, under the direction of King Gos, continued to hurl arrows and darts and spears and axes and huge stones upon the invaders, all without avail. The ground below was thickly covered with weapons, yet not one of the three before the gates had been injured in the slightest manner. When everything had been cast that was available and not a single weapon of any sort remained at hand, the amazed warriors saw the boy put his shoulder against the gates and burst asunder the huge staples that held the bars in place. A thousand of their men could not have accomplished this feat, yet the small, slight boy did it with seeming ease. The gates burst open, and Inga advanced into the city street and called upon King Gos to surrender.

But Gos was now as badly frightened as were his warriors. He and his men were accustomed to war and pillage and they had carried terror into many countries, but here was a small boy, a fat man and a goat who could not be injured by all his skill in warfare, his numerous army and thousands of death-dealing weapons. Moreover, they not only defied King Gos's entire army but they had broken in the huge gates of the city—as easily as if they had been made of paper —and such an exhibition of enormous strength

made the wicked King fear for his life. Like all
bullies and marauders, Gos was a coward at
heart, and now a panic seized him and he turned
and fled before the calm advance of Prince Inga
of Pingaree. The warriors were like their master,
and having thrown all their weapons over the
wall and being helpless to oppose the strangers,
they all swarmed after Gos, who abandoned his
city and crossed the bridge of boats to the Island
of Coregos. There was a desperate struggle
among these cowardly warriors to get over the
bridge, and many were pushed into the water
and obliged to swim; but finally every fighting

man of Regos had gained the shore of Coregos and then they tore away the bridge of boats and drew them up on their own side, hoping the stretch of open water would prevent the magic invaders from following them.

The humble citizens and serving people of Regos, who had been terrified and abused by the rough warriors all their lives, were not only greatly astonished by this sudden conquest of their masters but greatly delighted. As the King and his army fled to Coregos, the people embraced one another and danced for very joy, and then they turned to see what the conquerors of Regos were like.

Rinkitink Makes a Great Mistake

CHAPTER 8

THE fat King rode his
goat through the streets
of the conquered city
and the boy Prince
walked proudly beside
him, while all the people bent their heads
humbly to their new masters, whom they were
prepared to serve in the same manner they had
King Gos.

Not a warrior remained in all Regos to oppose
the triumphant three; the bridge of boats had
been destroyed; Inga and his companions were
free from danger—for a time, at least.

The jolly little King appreciated this fact and
rejoiced that he had escaped all injury during
the battle. How it had all happened he could
not tell, nor even guess, but he was content in

being safe and free to take possession of the enemy's city. So, as they passed through the lines of respectful civilians on their way to the palace, the King tipped his crown back on his bald head and folded his arms and sang in his best voice the following lines:

"Oh, here comes the army of King Rinkitink!
  It isn't a big one, perhaps you may think,
But it scattered the warriors quicker than wink—
    Rink-i-tink, tink-i-tink, tink!
Our Bilbil's a hero and so is his King;
Our foemen have vanished like birds on the
    wing;
I guess that as fighters we're quite the real
    thing—
    Rink-i-tink, tink-i-tink, tink!"

"Why don't you give a little credit to Inga?" inquired the goat. "If I remember aright, he did a little of the conquering himself."

"So he did," responded the King, "and that's the reason I'm sounding our own praise, Bilbil. Those who do the least, often shout the loudest and so get the most glory. Inga did so much that there is danger of his becoming more important than we are, and so we'd best say nothing about him."

When they reached the palace, which was

an immense building, furnished throughout in regal splendor, Inga took formal possession and ordered the majordomo to show them the finest rooms the building contained. There were many pleasant apartments, but Rinkitink proposed to Inga that they share one of the largest bedrooms together.

"For," said he, "we are not sure that old Gos will not return and try to recapture his city, and you must remember that I have no magic to protect me. In any danger, were I alone, I might be easily killed or captured, while if you are by my side you can save me from injury."

The boy realized the wisdom of this plan, and selected a fine big bedroom on the second floor of the palace, in which he ordered two golden beds placed and prepared for King Rinkitink and himself. Bilbil was given a suite of rooms on the other side of the palace, where servants brought the goat fresh-cut grass to eat and made him a soft bed to lie upon.

That evening the boy Prince and the fat King dined in great state in the lofty-domed dining-hall of the palace, where forty servants waited upon them. The royal chef, anxious to win the favor of the conquerors of Regos, prepared his finest and most savory dishes for them, which Rinkitink ate with much appetite and found so delicious that he ordered the royal chef brought

into the banquet hall and presented him with a gilt button which the King cut from his own jacket.

"You are welcome to it," said he to the chef, "because I have eaten so much that I cannot use that lower button at all."

Rinkitink was mightily pleased to live in a comfortable palace again and to dine at a well spread table. His joy grew every moment, so that he came in time to be as merry and cheery as before Pingaree was despoiled. And, although he had been much frightened during Inga's defiance of the army of King Gos, he now began to turn the matter into a joke.

"Why, my boy," said he, "you whipped the big black-bearded King exactly as if he were a schoolboy, even though you used no warlike weapon at all upon him. He was cowed through fear of your magic, and that reminds me to demand from you an explanation. How did you do it, Inga? And where did the wonderful magic come from?"

Perhaps it would have been wise for the Prince to have explained about the magic pearls, but at that moment he was not inclined to do so. Instead, he replied:

"Be patient, Your Majesty. The secret is not my own, so please do not ask me to divulge it. Is it not enough, for the present, that the magic saved you from death to-day?"

"Do not think me ungrateful," answered the King earnestly. "A million spears fell on me from the wall, and several stones as big as mountains, yet none of them hurt me!"

"The stones were not as big as mountains, sire," said the Prince with a smile. "They were, indeed, no larger than your head."

"Are you sure about that?" asked Rinkitink.

"Quite sure, Your Majesty."

"How deceptive those things are!" sighed the King. "This argument reminds me of the story of Tom Tick, which my father used to tell."

"I have never heard that story," Inga answered.

"Well, as he told it, it ran like this:

"When Tom walked out, the sky to spy,
    A naughty gnat flew in his eye;
    But Tom knew not it was a gnat—
    He thought, at first, it was a cat.

"And then, it felt so very big,
    He thought it surely was a pig
    Till, standing still to hear it grunt,
    He cried: 'Why, it's an *elephunt!*'

"But—when the gnat flew out again
    And Tom was free from all his pain,
    He said: 'There flew into my eye
    A leetle, teenty-tiny fly.' "

"Indeed," said Inga, laughing, "the gnat was much like your stones that seemed as big as mountains."

After their dinner they inspected the palace, which was filled with valuable goods stolen by King Gos from many nations. But the day's events had tired them and they retired early to their big sleeping apartment.

"In the morning," said the boy to Rinkitink, as he was undressing for bed, "I shall begin the search for my father and mother and the people of Pingaree. And, when they are found and rescued, we will all go home again, and be as happy as we were before."

They carefully bolted the door of their room, that no one might enter, and then got into their beds, where Rinkitink fell asleep in an instant. The boy lay awake for a while thinking over the day's adventures, but presently he fell sound asleep also, and so weary was he that nothing disturbed his slumber until he awakened next morning with a ray of sunshine in his eyes, which had crept into the room through the open window by King Rinkitink's bed.

Resolving to begin the search for his parents without any unnecessary delay, Inga at once got out of bed and began to dress himself, while Rinkitink, in the other bed, was still sleeping peacefully. But when the boy had put on both

his stockings and began looking for his shoes, he could find but one of them. The left shoe, that containing the Pink Pearl, was missing.

Filled with anxiety at this discovery, Inga searched through the entire room, looking underneath the beds and divans and chairs and behind the draperies and in the corners and every other possible place a shoe might be. He tried the door, and found it still bolted; so, with growing uneasiness, the boy was forced to admit that the precious shoe was not in the room.

With a throbbing heart he aroused his companion.

"King Rinkitink," said he, "do you know what has become of my left shoe?"

"Your shoe!" exclaimed the King, giving a wide yawn and rubbing his eyes to get the sleep out of them. "Have you lost a shoe?"

"Yes," said Inga. "I have searched everywhere in the room, and cannot find it."

"But why bother me about such a small thing?" inquired Rinkitink. "A shoe is only a shoe, and you can easily get another one. But, stay! Perhaps it was your shoe which I threw at the cat last night."

"The cat!" cried Inga. "What do you mean?"

"Why, in the night," explained Rinkitink, sitting up and beginning to dress himself, "I was wakened by the mewing of a cat that sat upon a wall of the palace, just outside my window. As the noise disturbed me, I reached out in the dark and caught up something and threw it at the cat, to frighten the creature away. I did not know what it was that I threw, and I was too sleepy to care; but probably it was your shoe, since it is now missing."

"Then," said the boy, in a despairing tone of voice, "your carelessness has ruined me, as well as yourself, King Rinkitink, for in that shoe was concealed the magic power which protected us from danger."

The King's face became very serious when he heard this and he uttered a low whistle of surprise and regret.

"Why on earth did you not warn me of this?" he demanded. "And why did you keep such a precious power in an old shoe? And why didn't you put the shoe under a pillow? You were very wrong, my lad, in not confiding to me, your faithful friend, the secret, for in that case the shoe would not now be lost."

To all this Inga had no answer. He sat on the side of his bed, with hanging head, utterly disconsolate, and seeing this, Rinkitink had pity for his sorrow.

"Come!" cried the King; "let us go out at once and look for the shoe which I threw at the cat. It must even now be lying in the yard of the palace."

This suggestion roused the boy to action. He at once threw open the door and in his stocking feet rushed down the staircase, closely followed by Rinkitink. But although they looked on both sides of the palace wall and in every possible crack and corner where a shoe might lodge, they failed to find it.

After a half hour's careful search the boy said sorrowfully:

"Someone must have passed by, as we slept, and taken the precious shoe, not knowing its value. To us, King Rinkitink, this will be a dreadful misfortune, for we are surrounded by dangers from which we have now no protection. Luckily I have the other shoe left, within which is the magic power that gives me strength; so all is not lost."

Then he told Rinkitink, in a few words, the secret of the wonderful pearls, and how he had recovered them from the ruins and hidden them in his shoes, and how they had enabled him to drive King Gos and his men from Regos and to capture the city. The King was much astonished, and when the story was concluded he said to Inga:

"What did you do with the other shoe?"

"Why, I left it in our bedroom," replied the boy.

"Then I advise you to get it at once," continued Rinkitink, "for we can ill afford to lose the second shoe, as well as the one I threw at the cat."

"You are right!" cried Inga, and they hastened back to their bedchamber.

On entering the room they found an old woman sweeping and raising a great deal of dust.

"Where is my shoe?" asked the Prince, anxiously.

The old woman stopped sweeping and looked at him in a stupid way, for she was not very intelligent.

"Do you mean the one odd shoe that was lying on the floor when I came in?" she finally asked.

"Yes—yes!" answered the boy. "Where is it? Tell me where it is!"

"Why, I threw it on the dust-heap, outside the back gate," said she, "for, it being but a single shoe, with no mate, it can be of no use to anyone."

"Show us the way to the dust-heap—at once!" commanded the boy, sternly, for he was greatly frightened by this new misfortune which threatened him.

The old woman hobbled away and they followed her, constantly urging her to hasten; but when they reached the dust-heap no shoe was to be seen.

"This is terrible!" wailed the young Prince, ready to weep at his loss. "We are now absolutely ruined, and at the mercy of our enemies. Nor shall I be able to liberate my dear father and mother."

"Well," replied Rinkitink, leaning against an old barrel and looking quite solemn, "the thing is certainly unlucky, any way we look at it. I suppose someone has passed along here and, seeing the shoe upon the dust-heap, has carried it away. But no one could know the magic power the shoe contains and so will not use it against us. I believe, Inga, we must now depend upon our wits to get us out of the scrape we are in."

With saddened hearts they returned to the palace, and entering a small room where no one could observe them or overhear them, the boy took the White Pearl from its silken bag and held it to his ear, asking:

"What shall I do now?"

"Tell no one of your loss," answered the Voice of the Pearl. "If your enemies do not know that you are powerless, they will fear you as much as ever. Keep your secret, be patient, and fear not!"

Inga heeded this advice and also warned Rinkitink to say nothing to anyone of the loss of the shoes and the powers they contained. He sent for the shoemaker of King Gos, who soon brought him a new pair of red leather shoes that fitted him quite well. When these had been put upon his feet, the Prince, accompanied by the King, started to walk through the city.

Wherever they went the people bowed low to the conqueror, although a few, remembering Inga's terrible strength, ran away in fear and trembling. They had been used to severe masters and did not yet know how they would be treated by King Gos's successor. There being no occasion for the boy to exercise the powers he had displayed the previous day, his present helplessness was not suspected by any of the citizens of Regos, who still considered him a wonderful magician.

Inga did not dare to fight his way to the mines, at present, nor could he try to conquer the Island of Coregos, where his mother was enslaved; so he set about the regulation of the City of Regos, and having established himself with great state in the royal palace he began to govern the people by kindness, having consideration for the most humble.

The King of Regos and his followers sent spies across to the island they had abandoned in their flight, and these spies returned with the news that the terrible boy conqueror was still occupying the city. Therefore none of them ventured to go back to Regos but continued to live upon the neighboring island of Coregos, where they passed the days in fear and trembling and sought to plot and plan ways how they might overcome the Prince of Pingaree and the fat King of Gilgad.

A Present for Zella

CHAPTER 9

NOW it so happened
that on the morning of
that same day when the
Prince of Pingaree suf-
fered the loss of his
priceless shoes, there chanced to pass along the
road that wound beside the royal palace a poor
charcoal-burner named Nikobob, who was about
to return to his home in the forest.

Nikobob carried an ax and a bundle of torches
over his shoulder and he walked with his eyes
to the ground, being deep in thought as to the
strange manner in which the powerful King Gos
and his city had been conquered by a boy Prince
who had come from Pingaree.

Suddenly the charcoal-burner espied a shoe

lying upon the ground, just beyond the high wall of the palace and directly in his path. He picked it up and, seeing it was a pretty shoe, although much too small for his own foot, he put it in his pocket.

Soon after, on turning a corner of the wall, Nikobob came to a dust-heap where, lying amidst a mass of rubbish, was another shoe—the mate to the one he had before found. This also he placed in his pocket, saying to himself:

"I have now a fine pair of shoes for my daughter Zella, who will be much pleased to find I have brought her a present from the city."

And while the charcoal-burner turned into the forest and trudged along the path toward his home, Inga and Rinkitink were still searching for the missing shoes. Of course, they could not know that Nikobob had found them, nor did the honest man think he had taken anything more than a pair of cast-off shoes which nobody wanted.

Nikobob had several miles to travel through the forest before he could reach the little log cabin where his wife, as well as his little daughter Zella, awaited his return, but he was used to long walks and tramped along the path whistling cheerfully to beguile the time.

Few people, as I said before, ever passed through the dark and tangled forests of Regos, except to go to the mines in the mountain be-

yond, for many dangerous creatures lurked in the wild jungles, and King Gos never knew, when he sent a messenger to the mines, whether he would reach there safely or not.

The charcoal-burner, however, knew the wild forest well, and especially this part of it lying between the city and his home. It was the favorite haunt of the ferocious beast Choggenmugger, dreaded by every dweller in the Island of Regos. Choggenmugger was so old that everyone thought it must have been there since the world was made, and each year of its life the huge scales that covered its body grew thicker and harder and its jaws grew wider and its teeth grew sharper and its appetite grew more keen than ever.

In former ages there had been many dragons in Regos, but Choggenmugger was so fond of dragons that he had eaten all of them long ago. There had also been great serpents and crocodiles in the forest marshes, but all had gone to feed the hunger of Choggenmugger. The people of Regos knew well there was no use opposing the Great Beast, so when one unfortunately met with it he gave himself up for lost.

All this Nikobob knew well, but fortune had always favored him in his journey through the forest, and although he had at times met many savage beasts and fought them with his sharp ax, he had never to this day encountered the terrible Choggenmugger. Indeed, he was not thinking of the Great Beast at all as he walked along, but suddenly he heard a crashing of broken trees and felt a trembling of the earth and saw the immense jaws of Choggenmugger opening before him. Then Nikobob gave himself up for lost and his heart almost ceased to beat.

He believed there was no way of escape. No one ever dared oppose Choggenmugger. But Nikobob hated to die without showing the monster, in some way, that he was eaten only under protest. So he raised his ax and brought it down upon the red, protruding tongue of the monster —and cut it clean off!

For a moment the charcoal-burner scarcely believed what his eyes saw, for he knew nothing of the pearls he carried in his pocket or the magic power they lent his arm. His success, however, encouraged him to strike again, and this time the huge scaly jaw of Choggenmugger was severed in twain and the beast howled in terrified rage.

Nikobob took off his coat, to give himself more freedom of action, and then he earnestly renewed the attack. But now the ax seemed blunted by the hard scales and made no impression upon them whatever. The creature advanced with glaring, wicked eyes, and Nikobob seized his coat under his arm and turned to flee.

That was foolish, for Choggenmugger could run like the wind. In a moment it overtook the

charcoal-burner and snapped its four rows of sharp teeth together. But they did not touch Nikobob, because he still held the coat in his grasp, close to his body, and in the coat pocket were Inga's shoes, and in the points of the shoes were the magic pearls. Finding himself uninjured, Nikobob put on his coat, again seized his ax, and in a short time had chopped Choggenmugger into many small pieces—a task that proved not only easy but very agreeable.

"I must be the strongest man in all the world!" thought the charcoal-burner, as he proudly resumed his way, "for Choggenmugger has been the terror of Regos since the world began, and I alone have been able to destroy the beast. Yet it is singular that never before did I discover how powerful a man I am."

He met no further adventure and at midday reached a little clearing in the forest where stood his humble cabin.

"Great news! I have great news for you," he shouted, as his wife and little daughter came to greet him. "King Gos has been conquered by a boy Prince from the far island of Pingaree, and I have this day—unaided—destroyed Choggenmugger by the might of my strong arm."

This was, indeed, great news. They brought Nikobob into the house and set him in an easy chair and made him tell everything he knew about the Prince of Pingaree and the fat King of

Gilgad, as well as the details of his wonderful fight with mighty Choggenmugger.

"And now, my daughter," said the charcoal-burner, when all his news had been related for at least the third time, "here is a pretty present I have brought you from the city."

With this he drew the shoes from the pocket of his coat and handed them to Zella, who gave him a dozen kisses in payment and was much pleased with her gift. The little girl had never worn shoes before, for her parents were too poor to buy her such luxuries, so now the possession of these, which were not much worn, filled the child's heart with joy. She admired the red leather and the graceful curl of the pointed toes. When she tried them on her feet, they fitted as well as if made for her.

All the afternoon, as she helped her mother with the housework, Zella thought of her pretty shoes. They seemed more important to her than the coming to Regos of the conquering Prince of Pingaree, or even the death of Choggenmugger.

When Zella and her mother were not working in the cabin, cooking or sewing, they often searched the neighboring forest for honey which the wild bees cleverly hid in hollow trees. The day after Nikobob's return, as they were starting out after honey, Zella decided to put on her new shoes, as they would keep the twigs that covered the ground from hurting her feet. She was used to the twigs, of course, but what is the use of having nice, comfortable shoes, if you do not wear them?

So she danced along, very happily, followed by her mother, and presently they came to a tree in which was a deep hollow. Zella thrust her hand and arm into the space and found that the tree was full of honey, so she began to dig it out with a wooden paddle. Her mother, who held the pail, suddenly cried in warning:

"Look out, Zella; the bees are coming!" and then the good woman ran fast toward the house to escape.

Zella, however, had no more than time to turn her head when a thick swarm of bees surrounded her, angry because they had caught her stealing their honey and intent on stinging the girl as a punishment. She knew her danger and expected to be badly injured by the multitude of stinging bees, but to her surprise the little creatures were unable to fly close enough to her to stick their dart-like stingers into her flesh. They swarmed about her in a dark cloud, and their angry buzzing was terrible to hear, yet the little girl remained unharmed.

When she realized this, Zella was no longer afraid but continued to ladle out the honey until she had secured all that was in the tree. Then she returned to the cabin, where her mother was weeping and bemoaning the fate of her darling child, and the good woman was greatly astonished to find Zella had escaped injury.

Again they went to the woods to search for honey, and although the mother always ran away whenever the bees came near them, Zella paid no attention to the creatures but kept at her work, so that before supper time came the pails were again filled to overflowing with delicious honey.

"With such good fortune as we have had this day," said her mother, "we shall soon gather enough honey for you to carry to Queen Cor." For it seems the wicked Queen was very fond of honey and it had been Zella's custom to go, once every year, to the City of Coregos, to carry the Queen a supply of sweet honey for her table. Usually she had but one pail.

"But now," said Zella, "I shall be able to carry two pailsful to the Queen, who will, I am sure, give me a good price for it."

"True," answered her mother, "and, as the boy Prince may take it into his head to conquer Coregos, as well as Regos, I think it best for you to start on your journey to Queen Cor to-morrow morning. Do you not agree with me, Nikobob?" she added, turning to her husband, the charcoal-burner, who was eating his supper.

"I agree with you," he replied. "If Zella must go to the City of Coregos, she may as well start to-morrow morning."

The Cunning of Queen Cor

CHAPTER 10

YOU may be sure the Queen of Coregos was not well pleased to have King Gos and all his warriors living in her city after they had fled from their own. They were savage natured and quarrelsome men at all times, and their tempers had not improved since their conquest by the Prince of Pingaree. Moreover, they were eating up Queen Cor's provisions and crowding the houses of her own people, who grumbled and complained until their Queen was heartily tired.

"Shame on you!" she said to her husband, King Gos, "to be driven out of your city by a boy, a roly-poly King and a billy goat! Why do you not go back and fight them?"

"No human can fight against the powers of magic," returned the King in a surly voice. "That boy is either a fairy or under the protection of fairies. We escaped with our lives only because we were quick to run away; but, should we return to Regos, the same terrible power that burst open the city gates would crush us all to atoms."

"Bah! you are a coward," cried the Queen, tauntingly.

"I am not a coward," said the big King. "I have killed in battle scores of my enemies; by the might of my sword and my good right arm I have conquered many nations; all my life people have feared me. But no one would dare face the tremendous power of the Prince of Pingaree, boy though he is. It would not be courage, it would be folly, to attempt it."

"Then meet his power with cunning," suggested the Queen. "Take my advice, and steal over to Regos at night, when it is dark, and capture or destroy the boy while he sleeps."

"No weapon can touch his body," was the answer. "He bears a charmed life and cannot be injured."

"Does the fat King possess magic powers, or the goat?" inquired Cor.

"I think not," said Gos. "We could not injure them, indeed, any more than we could the boy, but they did not seem to have any unusual strength, although the goat's head is harder than a battering-ram."

"Well," mused the Queen, "there is surely some way to conquer that slight boy. If you are afraid to undertake the job, I shall go myself. By some stratagem I shall manage to make him my prisoner. He will not dare to defy a Queen and no magic can stand against a woman's cunning."

"Go ahead, if you like," replied the King, with an evil grin, "and if you are hung up by the thumbs or cast into a dungeon, it will serve you right for thinking you can succeed where a skilled warrior dares not make the attempt."

"I'm not afraid," answered the Queen. "It is only soldiers and bullies who are cowards."

In spite of this assertion, Queen Cor was not so brave as she was cunning. For several days she thought over this plan and that, and tried to decide which was most likely to succeed. She had never seen the boy Prince but had heard so many tales of him from the defeated warriors, and especially from Captain Buzzub, that she had learned to respect his power.

Spurred on by the knowledge that she would never get rid of her unwelcome guests until Prince Inga was overcome and Regos regained for King Gos, the Queen of Coregos finally decided to trust to luck and her native wit to defeat a simple-minded boy, however powerful he might be. Inga could not suspect what she was going to do, because she did not know herself. She intended to act boldly and trust to chance to win.

It is evident that had the cunning Queen known that Inga had lost all his magic, she would not have devoted so much time to the simple matter of capturing him, but like all others she was impressed by the marvelous exhibition of power he had shown in capturing Regos, and had no reason to believe the boy was less powerful now.

One morning Queen Cor boldly entered a boat, and, taking four men with her as an escort and bodyguard, was rowed across the narrow channel to Regos. Prince Inga was sitting in the palace playing checkers with King Rinkitink when a servant came to him, saying that Queen Cor had arrived and desired an audience with him.

With many misgivings lest the wicked Queen discover that he had now lost his magic powers, the boy ordered her to be admitted, and she soon entered the room and bowed low before him, in mock respect.

Cor was a big woman, almost as tall as King Gos. She had flashing black eyes and the dark complexion you see on gypsies. Her temper, when irritated, was something dreadful, and her face wore an evil expression which she tried to cover by smiling sweetly—often when she meant the most mischief.

"I have come," said she in a low voice, "to render homage to the noble Prince of Pingaree. I am told that Your Highness is the strongest person in the world, and invincible in battle, and therefore I wish you to become my friend, rather than my enemy."

Now Inga did not know how to reply to this speech. He disliked the appearance of the woman and was afraid of her and he was unused to deception and did not know how to mask his real feelings. So he took time to think over his answer, which he finally made in these words:

"I have no quarrel with Your Majesty, and my only reason for coming here is to liberate my father and mother, and my people, whom you and your husband have made your slaves, and to recover the goods King Gos has plundered from the Island of Pingaree. This I hope soon to accomplish, and if you really wish to be my friend, you can assist me greatly."

While he was speaking Queen Cor had been studying the boy's face stealthily, from the corners of her eyes, and she said to herself: "He is so small and innocent that I believe I can capture him alone, and with ease. He does not seem very terrible and I suspect that King Gos and his warriors were frightened at nothing." Then, aloud, she said to Inga:

"I wish to invite you, mighty Prince, and your friend, the great King of Gilgad, to visit my poor palace at Coregos, where all my people shall do you honor. Will you come?"

"At present," replied Inga, uneasily, "I must refuse your kind invitation."

"There will be feasting, and dancing girls, and games and fireworks," said the Queen, speaking as if eager to entice him and at each word coming a step nearer to where he stood.

"I could not enjoy them while my poor parents are slaves," said the boy, sadly.

"Are you sure of that?" asked Queen Cor, and by that time she was close beside Inga. Suddenly she leaned forward and threw both of her long arms around Inga's body, holding him in a grasp that was like a vise.

Now Rinkitink sprang forward to rescue his friend, but Cor kicked out viciously with her foot and struck the King squarely on his stomach —a very tender place to be kicked, especially if one is fat. Then, still hugging Inga tightly, the Queen called aloud:

"I've got him! Bring in the ropes."

Instantly the four men she had brought with her sprang into the room and bound the boy hand and foot. Next they seized Rinkitink, who was still rubbing his stomach, and bound him likewise.

With a laugh of wicked triumph, Queen Cor

now led her captives down to the boat and returned with them to Coregos.

Great was the astonishment of King Gos and his warriors when they saw that the mighty Prince of Pingaree, who had put them all to flight, had been captured by a woman. Cowards as they were, they now crowded around the boy and jeered at him, and some of them would have struck him had not the Queen cried out:

"Hands off! He is my prisoner, remember— not yours."

"Well, Cor, what are you going to do with him?" inquired King Gos.

"I shall make him my slave, that he may amuse my idle hours. For he is a pretty boy, and gentle, although he did frighten all of you big warriors so terribly."

The King scowled at this speech, not liking to be ridiculed, but he said nothing more. He and his men returned that same day to Regos, after restoring the bridge of boats. And they held a wild carnival of rejoicing, both in the King's palace and in the city, although the poor people of Regos who were not warriors were all sorry that the kind young Prince had been captured by his enemies and could rule them no longer.

When her unwelcome guests had all gone back to Regos and the Queen was alone in her palace, she ordered Inga and Rinkitink brought before her and their bonds removed. They came sadly enough, knowing they were in serious straits and at the mercy of a cruel mistress. Inga had taken counsel of the White Pearl, which had advised him to bear up bravely under his misfortune, promising a change for the better very soon. With this promise to comfort him, Inga faced the Queen with a dignified bearing that indicated both pride and courage.

"Well, youngster," said she, in a cheerful tone because she was pleased with her success, "you played a clever trick on my poor husband and frightened him badly, but for that prank I am inclined to forgive you. Hereafter I intend you to be my page, which means that you must fetch and carry for me at my will. And let me advise you to obey my every whim without question or delay, for when I am angry I become ugly, and when I am ugly someone is sure to feel the lash. Do you understand me?"

Inga bowed, but made no answer. Then she turned to Rinkitink and said:

"As for you, I cannot decide how to make you useful to me, as you are altogether too fat and awkward to work in the fields. It may be, however, that I can use you as a pincushion."

"What!" cried Rinkitink in horror, "would you stick pins into the King of Gilgad?"

"Why not?" returned Queen Cor. "You are as fat as a pincushion, as you must yourself admit, and whenever I needed a pin I could call you to me." Then she laughed at his frightened look and asked: "By the way, are you ticklish?"

This was the question Rinkitink had been dreading. He gave a moan of despair and shook his head.

"I should love to tickle the bottom of your feet with a feather," continued the cruel woman. "Please take off your shoes."

"Oh, your Majesty!" pleaded poor Rinkitink, "I beg you to allow me to amuse you in some other way. I can dance, or I can sing you a song."

"Well," she answered, shaking with laughter, "you may sing a song—if it be a merry one. But you do not seem in a merry mood."

"I *feel* merry—indeed, Your Majesty, I do!" protested Rinkitink, anxious to escape the tickling. But even as he professed to "feel merry" his round, red face wore an expression of horror and anxiety that was really comical.

"Sing, then!" commanded Queen Cor, who was greatly amused.

Rinkitink gave a sigh of relief and after clearing his throat and trying to repress his sobs he began to sing this song—gently, at first, but finally roaring it out at the top of his voice:

"Oh!
There was a Baby Tiger lived in a men-ag-er-ie—

Fizzy-fezzy-fuzzy—they wouldn't set him free;
And ev'rybody thought that he was gentle as
could be—
Fizzy-fezzy-fuzzy—Ba-by Ti-ger!

"Oh!
They patted him upon his head and shook him
by the paw—
Fizzy-fezzy-fuzzy—he had a bone to gnaw;
But soon he grew the biggest Tiger that you ever
saw—
Fizzy-fezzy-fuzzy—what a Ti-ger!

"Oh!
One day they came to pet the brute and he began
to fight—
Fizzy-fezzy-fuzzy—how he did scratch and
bite!
He broke the cage and in a rage he darted out
of sight—
Fizzy-fezzy-fuzzy was a Ti-ger!"

"And is there a moral to the song?" asked Queen
Cor, when King Rinkitink had finished his song
with great spirit.

"If there is," replied Rinkitink, "it is a warning not to fool with tigers."

The little Prince could not help smiling at this
shrewd answer, but Queen Cor frowned and
gave the King a sharp look.

"Oh," said she; "I think I know the difference

between a tiger and a lapdog. But I'll bear the warning in mind, just the same."

For, after all her success in capturing them, she was a little afraid of these people who had once displayed such extraordinary powers.

Zella Goes to Coregos

CHAPTER 11

THE forest in which Nikobob lived with his wife and daughter stood between the mountains and the City of Regos, and a well-beaten path wound among the trees, leading from the city to the mines. This path was used by the King's messengers, and captured prisoners were also sent by this way from Regos to work in the underground caverns.

Nikobob had built his cabin more than a mile away from this path, that he might not be molested by the wild and lawless soldiers of King Gos, but the family of the charcoal-burner was surrounded by many creatures scarcely less dangerous to encounter, and often in the night they could hear savage animals growling and prowling about the cabin. Because Nikobob minded his own business and never hunted the wild creatures to injure them, the beasts had come to regard him as one of the natural dwellers in the forest and did not molest him or his family. Still Zella and her mother seldom wandered far from home, except on such errands as carrying honey to Coregos, and at these times Nikobob cautioned them to be very careful.

So when Zella set out on her journey to Queen Cor, with the two pails of honey in her hands, she was undertaking a dangerous adventure and there was no certainty that she would return safely to her loving parents. But they were poor, and Queen Cor's money, which they expected to receive for the honey, would enable them to purchase many things that were needed; so it was deemed best that Zella should go. She was a brave little girl and poor people are often obliged to take chances that rich ones are spared.

A passing woodchopper had brought news to Nikobob's cabin that Queen Cor had made a prisoner of the conquering Prince of Pingaree and that Gos and his warriors were again back in their city of Regos; but these struggles and conquests were matters which, however interesting, did not concern the poor charcoal-burner or his family. They were more anxious over the report that the warriors had become more reck-

less than ever before, and delighted in annoying all the common people; so Zella was told to keep away from the beaten path as much as possible, that she might not encounter any of the King's soldiers.

"When it is necessary to choose between the warriors and the wild beasts," said Nikobob, "the beasts will be found the more merciful."

The little girl had put on her best attire for the journey and her mother threw a blue silk shawl over her head and shoulders. Upon her feet were the pretty red shoes her father had brought her from Regos. Thus prepared, she kissed her parents good-bye and started out with a light heart, carrying the pails of honey in either hand.

It was necessary for Zella to cross the path that led from the mines to the city, but once on the other side she was not likely to meet with anyone, for she had resolved to cut through the forest and so reach the bridge of boats without entering the City of Regos, where she might be interrupted. For an hour or two she found the walking easy enough, but then the forest, which in this part was unknown to her, became badly tangled. The trees were thicker and creeping vines intertwined between them. She had to turn this way and that to get through at all, and finally she came to a place where a network of vines and branches effectually barred her farther progress.

Zella was dismayed, at first, when she encountered this obstacle, but setting down her pails she made an endeavor to push the branches aside. At her touch they parted as if by magic, breaking asunder like dried twigs, and she found she could pass freely. At another place a great log had fallen across her way, but the little girl lifted it easily and cast it aside, although six ordinary men could scarcely have moved it.

The child was somewhat worried at this evidence of a strength she had heretofore been ignorant that she possessed. In order to satisfy herself that it was no delusion, she tested her new-found power in many ways, finding that nothing was too big nor too heavy for her to lift. And, naturally enough, the girl gained courage from these experiments and became confident that she could protect herself in any emergency. When, presently, a wild boar ran toward her, grunting horribly and threatening her with its great tusks, she did not climb a tree to escape, as she had always done before on meeting such creatures, but stood still and faced the boar. When it had come quite close and Zella saw that it could not injure her—a fact that astonished both the beast and the girl—she suddenly reached down and seizing it by one ear

threw the great beast far off amongst the trees, where it fell headlong to the earth, grunting louder than ever with surprise and fear.

The girl laughed merrily at this incident and, picking up her pails, resumed her journey through the forest. It is not recorded whether the wild boar told his adventure to the other beasts or they had happened to witness his defeat, but certain it is that Zella was not again molested. A brown bear watched her pass without making any movement in her direction and a great puma—a beast much dreaded by all men—crept out of her path as she approached, and disappeared among the trees.

Thus everything favored the girl's journey and she made such good speed that by noon she emerged from the forest's edge and found she was quite near to the bridge of boats that led to Coregos. This she crossed safely and without meeting any of the rude warriors she so greatly feared, and five minutes later the daughter of the charcoal-burner was seeking admittance at the back door of Queen Cor's palace.

The Excitement of Bilbil the Goat

CHAPTER 12

OUR story must now return to one of our characters whom we have been forced to neglect. The temper of Bilbil the goat was not sweet under any circumstances, and whenever he had a grievance he was inclined to be quite grumpy. So, when his master settled down in the palace of King Gos for a quiet life with the boy Prince, and passed his time in playing checkers and eating and otherwise enjoying himself, he had no use whatever for Bilbil, and shut the goat in an upstairs room to prevent his wandering through the city and quarreling with the citizens. But this Bilbil did not like at all. He became very cross and disagreeable at being left alone and he did not speak nicely to the servants who came to bring him food; therefore those people decided not to wait upon him any more, resenting his conversation and not liking to be scolded by a lean, scraggly goat, even though it belonged to a conqueror. The servants kept away from the room and Bilbil grew more hungry and more angry every hour. He tried to eat the rugs and ornaments, but found them not at all nourishing. There was no grass to be had unless he escaped from the palace.

When Queen Cor came to capture Inga and Rinkitink, both the prisoners were so filled with despair at their own misfortune that they gave no thought whatever to the goat, who was left in his room. Nor did Bilbil know anything of the changed fortunes of his comrades until he heard shouts and boisterous laughter in the courtyard below. Looking out of a window, with the intention of rebuking those who dared thus to disturb him, Bilbil saw the courtyard quite filled with warriors and knew from this that the palace had in some way again fallen into the hands of the enemy.

Now, although Bilbil was often exceedingly disagreeable to King Rinkitink, as well as to the Prince, and sometimes used harsh words in addressing them, he was intelligent enough to know them to be his friends, and to know that

King Gos and his people were his foes. In sudden anger, provoked by the sight of the warriors and the knowledge that he was in the power of the dangerous men of Regos, Bilbil butted his head against the door of his room and burst it open. Then he ran to the head of the staircase and saw King Gos coming up the stairs followed by a long line of his chief captains and warriors.

The goat lowered his head, trembling with rage and excitement, and just as the King reached the top stair the animal dashed forward and butted His Majesty so fiercely that the big and powerful King, who did not expect an attack, doubled up and tumbled backward. His great weight knocked over the man just behind him and he in turn struck the next warrior and upset him, so that in an instant the whole line of Bilbil's foes was tumbling heels over head to the bottom of the stairs, where they piled up in a heap, struggling and shouting and in the mixup hitting one another with their fists, until every man of them was bruised and sore.

Finally King Gos scrambled out of the heap and rushed up the stairs again, very angry indeed. Bilbil was ready for him and a second time butted the King down the stairs; but now the goat also lost his balance and followed the King, landing full upon the confused heap of

soldiers. Then he kicked out so viciously with his heels that he soon freed himself and dashed out of the doorway of the palace.

"Stop him!" cried King Gos, running after.

But the goat was now so wild and excited that it was not safe for anyone to stand in his way. None of the men were armed and when one or two tried to head off the goat, Bilbil sent them sprawling upon the ground. Most of the warriors, however, were wise enough not to attempt to interfere with his flight.

Coursing down the street, Bilbil found himself approaching the bridge of boats and without pausing to think where it might lead him he crossed over and proceeded on his way. A few moments later a great stone building blocked his path. It was the palace of Queen Cor, and seeing the gates of the courtyard standing wide open, Bilbil rushed through them without slackening his speed.

Zella Saves the Prince

CHAPTER 13

THE wicked Queen of Coregos was in a very bad humor this morning, for one of her slave drivers had come from the fields to say that a number of slaves had rebelled and would not work.

"Bring them here to me!" she cried savagely. "A good whipping may make them change their minds."

So the slave driver went to fetch the rebellious ones and Queen Cor sat down to eat her breakfast, an ugly look on her face.

Prince Inga had been ordered to stand behind his new mistress with a big fan of peacock's feathers, but he was so unused to such service that he awkwardly brushed her ear with the fan. At once she flew into a terrible rage and slapped the Prince twice with her hand—blows that tingled, too, for her hand was big and hard and she was not inclined to be gentle. Inga took the blows without shrinking or uttering a cry, although they stung his pride far more than his body. But King Rinkitink, who was acting as the queen's butler and had just brought in her coffee, was so startled at seeing the young Prince punished that he tipped over the urn and the hot coffee streamed across the lap of the Queen's best morning gown.

Cor sprang from her seat with a scream of anger and poor Rinkitink would doubtless have been given a terrible beating had not the slave driver returned at this moment and attracted the woman's attention. The overseer had brought with him all of the women slaves from Pingaree, who had been loaded down with chains and were so weak and ill they could scarcely walk, much less work in the fields.

Prince Inga's eyes were dimmed with sorrowful tears when he discovered how his poor people had been abused, but his own plight was so helpless that he was unable to aid them. Fortunately the boy's mother, Queen Garee, was not among these slaves, for Queen Cor had placed her in the royal dairy to make butter.

"Why do you refuse to work?" demanded

Cor in a harsh voice, as the slaves from Pingaree stood before her, trembling and with downcast eyes.

"Because we lack strength to perform the tasks your overseers demand," answered one of the women.

"Then you shall be whipped until your strength returns!" exclaimed the Queen, and turning to Inga, she commanded: "Get me the whip with the seven lashes."

As the boy left the room, wondering how he might manage to save the unhappy women from their undeserved punishment, he met a girl entering by the back way, who asked:

"Can you tell me where to find Her Majesty, Queen Cor?"

"She is in the chamber with the red dome, where green dragons are painted upon the walls," replied Inga; "but she is in an angry and ungracious mood to-day. Why do you wish to see her?"

"I have honey to sell," answered the girl, who was Zella, just come from the forest. "The Queen is very fond of my honey."

"You may go to her, if you so desire," said the boy, "but take care not to anger the cruel Queen, or she may do you a mischief."

"Why should she harm me, who brings her the honey she so dearly loves?" inquired the child innocently. "But I thank you for your warning; and I will try not to anger the Queen."

As Zella started to go, Inga's eyes suddenly fell upon her shoes and instantly he recognized them as his own. For only in Pingaree were shoes shaped in this manner: high at the heel and pointed at the toes.

"Stop!" he cried in an excited voice, and the girl obeyed, wonderingly. "Tell me," he continued, more gently, "where did you get those shoes?"

"My father brought them to me from Regos," she answered.

"From Regos!"

"Yes. Are they not pretty?" asked Zella, looking down at her feet to admire them. "One of them my father found by the palace wall, and the other on an ash-heap. So he brought them to me and they fit me perfectly."

By this time Inga was trembling with eager joy, which of course the girl could not understand.

"What is your name, little maid?" he asked.

"I am called Zella, and my father is Nikobob, the charcoal-burner."

"Zella is a pretty name. I am Inga, Prince of Pingaree," said he, "and the shoes you are now wearing, Zella, belong to me. They were not cast away, as your father supposed, but were lost. Will you let me have them again?"

Zella's eyes filled with tears.

"Must I give up my pretty shoes, then?" she asked. "They are the only ones I have ever owned."

Inga was sorry for the poor child, but he knew how important it was that he regain possession of the Magic Pearls. So he said, pleadingly:

"Please let me have them, Zella. See! I will exchange for them the shoes I now have on, which are newer and prettier than the others."

The girl hesitated. She wanted to please the boy Prince, yet she hated to exchange the shoes which her father had brought her as a present.

"If you will give me the shoes," continued the boy, anxiously, "I will promise to make you and your father and mother rich and prosperous. Indeed, I will promise to grant any favors you may ask of me," and he sat down upon the floor and drew off the shoes he was wearing and held them toward the girl.

"I'll see if they will fit me," said Zella, taking off her left shoe—the one that contained the Pink Pearl—and beginning to put on one of Inga's.

Just then Queen Cor, angry at being made to wait for her whip with the seven lashes, rushed into the room to find Inga. Seeing the boy sitting upon the floor beside Zella, the woman sprang toward him to beat him with her clenched fists; but Inga had now slipped on the shoe and the Queen's blows could not reach his body.

Then Cor espied the whip lying beside Inga and snatching it up she tried to lash him with it —all to no avail.

While Zella sat horrified by this scene, the Prince, who realized he had no time to waste, reached out and pulled the right shoe from the girl's foot, quickly placing it upon his own. Then he stood up and, facing the furious but astonished Queen, said to her in a quiet voice:

"Madam, please give me that whip."

"I won't!" answered Cor. "I'm going to lash those Pingaree women with it."

The boy seized hold of the whip and with irresistible strength drew it from the Queen's hand. But she drew from her bosom a sharp dagger and with the swiftness of lightning aimed a blow at Inga's heart. He merely stood still and smiled, for the blade rebounded and fell clattering to the floor.

Then, at last, Queen Cor understood the magic power that had terrified her husband but which she had ridiculed in her ignorance, not believing in it. She did not know that Inga's power had been lost, and found again, but she realized the boy was no common foe and that unless she could still manage to outwit him her reign in the Island of Coregos was ended. To gain time, she went back to the red-domed chamber and seated herself in her throne, before which were grouped the weeping slaves from Pingaree.

Inga had taken Zella's hand and assisted her to put on the shoes he had given her in exchange for his own. She found them quite comfortable and did not know she had lost anything by the transfer.

"Come with me," then said the boy Prince, and led her into the presence of Queen Cor, who was giving Rinkitink a scolding. To the overseer Inga said:

"Give me the keys which unlock these chains, that I may set these poor women at liberty."

"Don't you do it!" screamed Queen Cor.

"If you interfere, madam," said the boy, "I will put you into a dungeon."

By this Rinkitink knew that Inga had recovered his Magic Pearls and the little fat King was so overjoyed that he danced and capered all around the room. But the Queen was alarmed at the threat and the slave driver, fearing the conqueror of Regos, tremblingly gave up the keys.

Inga quickly removed all the shackles from the women of his country and comforted them, telling them they should work no more but would soon be restored to their homes in Pingaree. Then he commanded the slave driver to go and get all the children who had been made slaves, and to bring them to their mothers. The man obeyed and left at once to perform his errand, while Queen Cor, growing more and more uneasy, suddenly sprang from her throne and before Inga could stop her had rushed through the room and out into the courtyard of the palace, meaning to make her escape. Rinkitink followed her, running as fast as he could go.

It was at this moment that Bilbil, in his mad dash from Regos, turned in at the gates of the courtyard, and as he was coming one way and Queen Cor was going the other they bumped into each other with great force. The woman sailed through the air, over Bilbil's head, and landed on the ground outside the gates, where her crown rolled into a ditch and she picked herself up, half dazed, and continued her flight. Bilbil was also somewhat dazed by the unexpected encounter, but he continued his rush rather blindly and so struck poor Rinkitink, who was chasing after Queen Cor. They rolled over one another a few times and then Rinkitink sat up and Bilbil sat up and they looked at each other in amazement.

"Bilbil," said the King, "I'm astonished at you!"

"Your Majesty," said Bilbil, "I expected kinder treatment at your hands."

"You interrupted me," said Rinkitink.

"There was plenty of room without your taking my path," declared the goat.

And then Inga came running out and said: "Where is the Queen?"

"Gone," replied Rinkitink, "but she cannot go far, as this is an island. However, I have found Bilbil, and our party is again reunited. You have recovered your magic powers, and again we are masters of the situation. So let us be thankful."

Saying this, the good little King got upon his feet and limped back into the throne room to help comfort the women.

Presently the children of Pingaree, who had been gathered together by the overseer, were brought in and restored to their mothers, and there was great rejoicing among them, you may be sure.

"But where is Queen Garee, my dear mother?" questioned Inga; but the women did not know and it was some time before the overseer remembered that one of the slaves from Pingaree had been placed in the royal dairy. Perhaps this was the woman the boy was seeking.

Inga at once commanded him to lead the way to the butter house, but when they arrived there Queen Garee was nowhere in the place, although the boy found a silk scarf which he recognized as one that his mother used to wear. Then they began a search throughout the island of Coregos, but could not find Inga's mother anywhere.

When they returned to the palace of Queen

Cor, Rinkitink discovered that the bridge of boats had again been removed, separating them from Regos, and from this they suspected that Queen Cor had fled to her husband's island and had taken Queen Garee with her. Inga was much perplexed what to do and returned with his friends to the palace to talk the matter over.

Zella was now crying because she had not sold her honey and was unable to return to her parents on the island of Regos, but the boy Prince comforted her and promised she should be protected until she could be restored to her home. Rinkitink found Queen Cor's purse, which she had had no time to take with her, and gave Zella several gold pieces for the honey. Then Inga ordered the palace servants to prepare a feast for all the women and children of Pingaree and to prepare for them beds in the great

palace, which was large enough to accommodate them all.

Then the boy and the goat and Rinkitink and Zella went into a private room to consider what should be done next.

The Escape

CHAPTER 14

"OUR fault," said Rink-
itink, "is that we con-
quer only one of these
twin islands at a time.
When we conquered
Regos, our foes all came to Coregos, and now
that we have conquered Coregos, the Queen
has fled to Regos. And each time they removed
the bridge of boats, so that we could not follow them."

"What has become of our own boat, in which
we came from Pingaree?" asked Bilbil.

"We left it on the shore of Regos," replied
the Prince, "but I wonder if we could not get it
again."

"Why don't you ask the White Pearl?" suggested Rinkitink.

"That is a good idea," returned the boy, and at once he drew the White Pearl from its silken bag and held it to his ear. Then he asked: "How may I regain our boat?"

The Voice of the Pearl replied: "Go to the south end of the Island of Coregos, and clap your hands three times and the boat will come to you."

"Very good!" cried Inga, and then he turned to his companions and said: "We shall be able to get our boat whenever we please; but what then shall we do?"

"Take me home in it!" pleaded Zella.

"Come with me to my City of Gilgad," said the King, "where you will be very welcome to remain forever."

"No," answered Inga, "I must rescue my father and mother, as well as my people. Already I have the women and children of Pingaree, but the men are with my father in the mines of Regos, and my dear mother has been taken away by Queen Cor. Not until all are rescued will I consent to leave these islands."

"Quite right!" exclaimed Bilbil.

"On second thought," said Rinkitink, "I agree with you. If you are careful to sleep in your shoes, and never take them off again, I believe you will be able to perform the task you have undertaken."

They counseled together for a long time as to

their mode of action and it was finally considered best to make the attempt to liberate King Kitticut first of all, and with him the men from Pingaree. This would give them an army to assist them and afterward they could march to Regos and compel Queen Cor to give up the Queen of Pingaree. Zella told them that they could go in their boat along the shore of Regos to a point opposite the mines, thus avoiding any conflict with the warriors of King Gos.

This being considered the best course to pursue, they resolved to start on the following morning, as night was even now approaching. The servants being all busy in caring for the women and children, Zella undertook to get a dinner for Inga and Rinkitink and herself and soon prepared a fine meal in the palace kitchen, for she was a good little cook and had often helped her mother. The dinner was served in a small room overlooking the gardens and Rinkitink thought the best part of it was the sweet honey, which he spread upon the biscuits that Zella had made. As for Bilbil, he wandered through the palace grounds and found some grass that made him a good dinner.

During the evening Inga talked with the women and cheered them, promising soon to reunite them with their husbands who were working in the mines and to send them back to their own island of Pingaree.

Next morning the boy rose bright and early and found that Zella had already prepared a nice breakfast. And after the meal they went to the most southern point of the island, which was not very far away, Rinkitink riding upon Bilbil's back and Inga and Zella following behind them, hand in hand.

When they reached the water's edge the boy advanced and clapped his hands together three times, as the White Pearl had told him to do. And in a few moments they saw in the distance the black boat with the silver lining, coming swiftly toward them from the sea. Presently it grounded on the beach and they all got into it. Zella was delighted with the boat, which was the most beautiful she had ever seen, and the marvel of its coming to them through the water without anyone to row it, made her a little afraid of the fairy craft. But Inga picked up the oars and began to row and at once the boat shot swiftly in the direction of Regos. They rounded the point of that island where the city was built and noticed that the shore was lined with warriors who had discovered their boat but seemed undecided whether to pursue it or not. This was probably because they had received no commands what to do, or perhaps they had learned to fear the magic powers of these adventurers from Pingaree and were unwilling to attack them unless their King ordered them to.

The Escape

The coast on the western side of the Island of Regos was very uneven and Zella, who knew fairly well the location of the mines from the inland forest path, was puzzled to decide which mountain they now viewed from the sea was the one where the entrance to the underground caverns was located. First she thought it was this peak, and then she guessed it was that; so considerable time was lost through her uncertainty.

They finally decided to land and explore the country, to see where they were, so Inga ran the boat into a little rocky cove where they all disembarked. For an hour they searched for the path without finding any trace of it and now Zella believed they had gone too far to the north and must return to another mountain that was nearer to the city.

Once again they entered the boat and followed the winding coast south until they thought they had reached the right place. By this time, however, it was growing dark, for the entire day had been spent in the search for the entrance to the mines, and Zella warned them that it would be safer to spend the night in the boat than on the land, where wild beasts were sure to disturb them. None of them realized at this time how fatal this day of search had been to their plans and perhaps if Inga had realized what was going on he would have landed and fought all the wild beasts in the forest rather than quietly remain in the boat until morning.

However, knowing nothing of the cunning plans of Queen Cor and King Gos, they anchored their boat in a little bay and cheerfully ate their dinner, finding plenty of food and drink in the boat's lockers. In the evening the stars came out in the sky and tipped the waves around their boat with silver. All around them was delightfully still save for the occasional snarl of a beast on the neighboring shore.

They talked together quietly of their adventures and their future plans and Zella told them her simple history and how hard her poor father was obliged to work, burning charcoal to sell for enough money to support his wife and child. Nikobob might be the humblest man in all Regos, but Zella declared he was a good man, and honest, and it was not his fault that his country was ruled by so wicked a King.

Then Rinkitink, to amuse them, offered to sing a song, and although Bilbil protested in his gruff way, claiming that his master's voice was cracked and disagreeable, the little King was encouraged by the others to sing his song, which he did.

"A red-headed man named Ned was dead;
    Sing fiddle-cum-faddle-cum-fi-do!

In battle he had lost his head;
    Sing fiddle-cum-faddle-cum-fi-do!
'Alas, poor Ned,' to him I said,
'How did you lose your head so red?'
    Sing fiddle-cum-faddle-cum-fi-do!

"Said Ned: 'I for my country bled,'
    Sing fiddle-cum-faddle-cum-fi-do!
'Instead of dying safe in bed',
    Sing fiddle-cum-faddle-cum-fi-do!
'If I had only fled, instead,
I then had been a head ahead.'
    Sing fiddle-cum-faddle-cum-fi-do!

"I said to Ned———"

"Do stop, Your Majesty!" pleaded Bilbil. "You're making my head ache."

"But the song isn't finished," replied Rinki-tink, "and as for your head aching, think of poor Ned, who hadn't any head at all!"

"I can think of nothing but your dismal singing," retorted Bilbil. "Why didn't you choose a cheerful subject, instead of telling how a man who was dead lost his red head? Really, Rinki-tink, I'm surprised at you."

"I know a splendid song about a live man," said the King.

"Then don't sing it," begged Bilbil.

Zella was both astonished and grieved by the

disrespectful words of the goat, for she had quite enjoyed Rinkitink's singing and had been taught a proper respect for Kings and those high in authority. But as it was now getting late they decided to go to sleep, that they might rise early the following morning, so they all reclined upon the bottom of the big boat and covered themselves with blankets which they found stored underneath the seats for just such occasions. They were not long in falling asleep and did not waken until daybreak.

After a hurried breakfast, for Inga was eager to liberate his father, the boy rowed the boat ashore and they all landed and began searching for the path. Zella found it within the next half hour and declared they must be very close to the entrance to the mines; so they followed the path toward the north, Inga going first, and then Zella following him, while Rinkitink brought up the rear riding upon Bilbil's back.

Before long they saw a great wall of rock towering before them, in which was a low arched entrance, and on either side of this entrance stood a guard, armed with a sword and a spear. The guards of the mines were not so fierce as the warriors of King Gos, their duty being to make the slaves work at their tasks and guard them from escaping; but they were as cruel as their cruel master wished them to be, and as cowardly as they were cruel.

Inga walked up to the two men at the entrance and said:

"Does this opening lead to the mines of King Gos?"

"It does," replied one of the guards, "but no one is allowed to pass out who once goes in."

"Nevertheless," said the boy, "we intend to go in and we shall come out whenever it pleases us to do so. I am the Prince of Pingaree, and I have come to liberate my people, whom King Gos has enslaved."

Now when the two guards heard this speech they looked at one another and laughed, and one of them said: "The King was right, for he said the boy was likely to come here and that he would try to set his people free. Also the King commanded that we must keep the little Prince in the mines, and set him to work, together with his companions."

"Then let us obey the King," replied the other man.

Inga was surprised at hearing this, and asked: "When did King Gos give you this order?"

"His Majesty was here in person last night," replied the man, "and went away again but an hour ago. He suspected you were coming here and told us to capture you if we could."

This report made the boy very anxious, not for himself but for his father, for he feared the King was up to some mischief. So he hastened

to enter the mines and the guards did nothing to oppose him or his companions, their orders being to allow him to go in but not to come out.

The little group of adventurers passed through a long rocky corridor and reached a low, wide cavern where they found a dozen guards and a hundred slaves, the latter being hard at work with picks and shovels digging for gold, while the guards stood over them with long whips.

Inga found many of the men from Pingaree among these slaves, but King Kitticut was not in this cavern; so they passed through it and entered another corridor that led to a second cavern. Here also hundreds of men were working, but the boy did not find his father amongst them, and so went on to a third cavern.

The corridors all slanted downward, so that the farther they went the lower into the earth they descended, and now they found the air hot and close and difficult to breathe. Flaming torches were stuck into the walls to give light to the workers, and these added to the oppressive heat.

The third and lowest cavern was the last in the mines, and here were many scores of slaves and many guards to keep them at work. So far, none of the guards had paid any attention to Inga's party, but allowed them to proceed as they would, and while the slaves cast curious glances at the boy and girl and man and goat, they dared say nothing. But now the boy walked up to some of the men of Pingaree and asked news of his father, telling them not to fear the guards as he would protect them from the whips.

Then he learned that King Kitticut had indeed been working in this very cavern until the evening before, when King Gos had come and taken him away—still loaded with chains.

"Seems to me," said King Rinkitink, when he heard this report, "that Gos has carried your father away to Regos, to prevent us from rescuing him. He may hide poor Kitticut in a dungeon, where we cannot find him."

"Perhaps you are right," answered the boy, "but I am determined to find him, wherever he may be."

Inga spoke firmly and with courage, but he was greatly disappointed to find that King Gos had been before him at the mines and had taken his father away. However, he tried not to feel disheartened, believing he would succeed in the end, in spite of all opposition. Turning to the guards, he said:

"Remove the chains from these slaves and set them free."

The guards laughed at this order, and one of them brought forward a handful of chains, saying: "His Majesty has commanded us to make you, also, a slave, for you are never to leave these caverns again."

Then he attempted to place the chains on
Inga, but the boy indignantly seized them and
broke them apart as easily as if they had been
cotton cords. When a dozen or more of the
guards made a dash to capture him, the Prince
swung the end of the chain like a whip and
drove them into a corner, where they cowered
and begged for mercy.

Stories of the marvelous strength of the boy
Prince had already spread to the mines of
Regos, and although King Gos had told them
that Inga had been deprived of all his magic
power, the guards now saw this was not true, so
they deemed it wise not to attempt to oppose
him.

The chains of the slaves had all been riveted
fast to their ankles and wrists, but Inga broke
the bonds of steel with his hands and set the
poor men free—not only those from Pingaree but
all who had been captured in the many wars and
raids of King Gos. They were very grateful, as
you may suppose, and agreed to support Prince
Inga in whatever action he commanded.

He led them to the middle cavern, where all
the guards and overseers fled in terror at his
approach, and soon he had broken apart the
chains of the slaves who had been working in
that part of the mines. Then they approached
the first cavern and liberated all there.

The slaves had been treated so cruelly by the

servants of King Gos that they were eager to
pursue and slay them, in revenge; but Inga held
them back and formed them into companies,
each company having its own leader. Then he
called the leaders together and instructed them
to march in good order along the path to the
City of Regos, where he would meet them and
tell them what to do next.

They readily agreed to obey him, and, arm-
ing themselves with iron bars and pick-axes
which they brought from the mines, the slaves
began their march to the city.

Zella at first wished to be left behind, that she
might make her way to her home, but neither
Rinkitink nor Inga thought it was safe for her to
wander alone through the forest, so they induced her to return with them to the city.

The boy beached his boat this time at the
same place as when he first landed at Regos, and
while many of the warriors stood on the shore
and before the walls of the city, not one of them
attempted to interfere with the boy in any way.
Indeed, they seemed uneasy and anxious, and
when Inga met Captain Buzzub the boy asked if
anything had happened in his absence.

"A great deal has happened," replied Buzzub.
"Our King and Queen have run away and left
us, and we don't know what to do."

"Run away!" exclaimed Inga. "Where did
they go to?"

"Who knows?" said the man, shaking his head despondently. "They departed together a few hours ago, in a boat with forty rowers, and they took with them the King and Queen of Pingaree!"

The Flight of the Rulers

CHAPTER 15

NOW it seems that when Queen Cor fled from her island to Regos, she had wit enough, although greatly frightened, to make a stop at the royal dairy, which was near to the bridge, and to drag poor Queen Garee from the butter-house and across to Regos with her. The warriors of King Gos had never before seen the terrible Queen Cor frightened, and therefore when she came running across the bridge of boats, dragging the Queen of Pingaree after her by one arm, the woman's great fright had the effect of terrifying the waiting warriors.

"Quick!" cried Cor. "Destroy the bridge, or we are lost."

While the men were tearing away the bridge

of boats the Queen ran up to the palace of Gos, where she met her husband.

"That boy is a wizard!" she gasped. "There is no standing against him."

"Oh, have you discovered his magic at last?" replied Gos, laughing in her face. "Who, now, is the coward?"

"Don't laugh!" cried Queen Cor. "It is no laughing matter. Both our islands are as good as conquered, this very minute. What shall we do, Gos?"

"Come in," he said, growing serious, "and let us talk it over."

So they went into a room of the palace and talked long and earnestly.

"The boy intends to liberate his father and mother, and all the people of Pingaree, and to take them back to their island," said Cor. "He may also destroy our palaces and make us his slaves. I can see but one way, Gos, to prevent him from doing all this, and whatever else he pleases to do."

"What way is that?" asked King Gos.

"We must take the boy's parents away from here as quickly as possible. I have with me the Queen of Pingaree, and you can run up to the mines and get the King. Then we will carry them away in a boat and hide them where the boy cannot find them, with all his magic. We will use the King and Queen of Pingaree as

hostages, and send word to the boy wizard that if he does not go away from our islands and allow us to rule them undisturbed, in our own way, we will put his father and mother to death. Also we will say that as long as we are let alone his parents will be safe, although still safely hidden. I believe, Gos, that in this way we can compel Prince Inga to obey us, for he seems very fond of his parents."

"It isn't a bad idea," said Gos, reflectively; "but where can we hide the King and Queen, so that the boy cannot find them?"

"In the country of the Nome King, on the mainland away at the south," she replied. "The nomes are our friends, and they possess magic powers that will enable them to protect the prisoners from discovery. If we can manage to get the King and Queen of Pingaree to the Nome Kingdom before the boy knows what we are doing, I am sure our plot will succeed."

Gos gave the plan considerable thought in the next five minutes, and the more he thought about it the more clever and reasonable it seemed. So he agreed to do as Queen Cor suggested and at once hurried away to the mines, where he arrived before Prince Inga did. The next morning he carried King Kitticut back to Regos.

While Gos was gone, Queen Cor busied herself in preparing a large and swift boat for the journey. She placed in it several bags of gold and jewels with which to bribe the nomes, and selected forty of the strongest oarsmen in Regos to row the boat. The instant King Gos returned with his royal prisoner all was ready for departure. They quickly entered the boat with their two important captives and without a word of explanation to any of their people they commanded the oarsmen to start, and were soon out of sight upon the broad expanse of the Nonestic Ocean.

Inga arrived at the city some hours later and was much distressed when he learned that his father and mother had been spirited away from the islands.

"I shall follow them, of course," said the boy to Rinkitink, "and if I cannot overtake them on the ocean I will search the world over until I find them. But before I leave here I must arrange to send our people back to Pingaree."

Nikobob Refuses a Crown

CHAPTER 16

ALMOST the first persons that Zella saw when she landed from the silver-lined boat at Regos were her father and mother. Nikobob and his wife had been greatly worried when their little daughter failed to return from Coregos, so they had set out to discover what had become of her. When they reached the City of Regos, that very morning, they were astonished to hear news of all the strange events that had taken place; still, they found comfort when told that Zella had been seen in the boat of Prince Inga, which had gone to the north. Then, while they wondered what this could mean, the silver-lined boat appeared again, with their daughter in it, and they ran down to the shore to give her a welcome and many joyful kisses.

Inga invited the good people to the palace of King Gos, where he conferred with them, as well as with Rinkitink and Bilbil.

"Now that the King and Queen of Regos and Coregos have run away," he said, "there is no one to rule these islands. So it is my duty to appoint a new ruler, and as Nikobob, Zella's father, is an honest and worthy man, I shall make him the King of the Twin Islands."

"Me?" cried Nikobob, astounded by this speech. "I beg Your Highness, on my bended knees, not to do so cruel a thing as to make me King!"

"Why not?" inquired Rinkitink. "I'm a King, and I know how it feels. I assure you, good Nikobob, that I quite enjoy my high rank, although a jeweled crown is rather heavy to wear in hot weather."

"With you, noble sir, it is different," said Nikobob, "for you are far from your kingdom and its trials and worries and may do as you please. But to remain in Regos, as King over these fierce and unruly warriors, would be to live in constant anxiety and peril, and the chances are that they would murder me within a month. As I have done no harm to anyone and have tried to be a good and upright man, I do not

think that I should be condemned to such a dreadful fate."

"Very well," replied Inga, "we will say no more about your being King. I merely wanted to make you rich and prosperous, as I had promised Zella."

"Please forget that promise," pleaded the charcoal-burner, earnestly; "I have been safe from molestation for many years, because I was poor and possessed nothing that anyone else could envy. But if you make me rich and prosperous I shall at once become the prey of thieves and marauders and probably will lose my life in the attempt to protect my fortune."

Inga looked at the man in surprise.

"What, then, can I do to please you?" he inquired.

"Nothing more than to allow me to go home to my poor cabin," said Nikobob.

"Perhaps," remarked King Rinkitink, "the charcoal-burner has more wisdom concealed in that hard head of his than we gave him credit for. But let us use that wisdom, for the present, to counsel us what to do in this emergency."

"What you call my wisdom," said Nikobob, "is merely common sense. I have noticed that some men become rich, and are scorned by some and robbed by others. Other men become famous, and are mocked at and derided by their fellows. But the poor and humble man who lives unnoticed and unknown escapes all these troubles and is the only one who can appreciate the joy of living."

"If I had a hand, instead of a cloven hoof, I'd like to shake hands with you, Nikobob," said Bilbil the goat. "But the poor man must not have a cruel master, or he is undone."

During the council they found, indeed, that the advice of the charcoal-burner was both shrewd and sensible, and they profited much by his words.

Inga gave Captain Buzzub the command of the warriors and made him promise to keep his men quiet and orderly—if he could. Then the boy allowed all of King Gos's former slaves, except those who came from Pingaree, to choose what boats they required and to stock them with provisions and row away to their own countries. When these had departed, with grateful thanks and many blessings showered upon the boy Prince who had set them free, Inga made preparations to send his own people home, where they were told to rebuild their houses and then erect a new royal palace. They were then to await patiently the coming of King Kitticut or Prince Inga.

"My greatest worry," said the boy to his friends, "is to know whom to appoint to take charge of this work of restoring Pingaree to its former condition. My men are all pearl fishers, and although willing and honest, have no talent for directing others how to work."

While the preparations for departure were being made, Nikobob offered to direct the men of Pingaree, and did so in a very capable manner. As the island had been despoiled of all its valuable furniture and draperies and rich cloths and paintings and statuary and the like, as well as gold and silver and ornaments, Inga thought it no more than just that they be replaced by the spoilers. So he directed his people to search through the storehouses of King Gos and to regain all their goods and chattels that could be found. Also he instructed them to take as much else as they required to make their new homes comfortable, so that many boats were loaded full of goods that would enable the people to restore Pingaree to its former state of comfort.

For his father's new palace the boy plundered the palaces of both Queen Cor and King Gos, sending enough wares away with his people to make King Kitticut's new residence as handsomely fitted and furnished as had been the one which the ruthless invaders from Regos had destroyed.

It was a great fleet of boats that set out one bright, sunny morning on the voyage to Pingaree, carrying all the men, women and children and all the goods for refitting their homes. As he saw the fleet depart, Prince Inga felt that

he had already successfully accomplished a part of his mission, but he vowed he would never return to Pingaree in person until he could take his father and mother there with him; unless, indeed, King Gos wickedly destroyed his beloved parents, in which case Inga would become the King of Pingaree and it would be his duty to go to his people and rule over them.

It was while the last of the boats were preparing to sail for Pingaree that Nikobob, who had been of great service in getting them ready, came to Inga in a thoughtful mood and said:

"Your Highness, my wife and my daughter Zella have been urging me to leave Regos and settle down in your island, in a new home. From what your people have told me, Pingaree is a better place to live than Regos, and there are no cruel warriors or savage beasts there to keep one in constant fear for the safety of those he loves. Therefore, I have come to ask to go with my family in one of the boats."

Inga was much pleased with this proposal and not only granted Nikobob permission to go to Pingaree to live, but instructed him to take with him sufficient goods to furnish his new home in a comfortable manner. In addition to this, he appointed Nikobob general manager of the buildings and of the pearl fisheries, until his father or he himself arrived, and the people approved this order because they liked Nikobob and knew him to be just and honest.

As soon as the last boat of the great flotilla had disappeared from the view of those left at Regos, Inga and Rinkitink prepared to leave the island themselves. The boy was anxious to overtake the boat of King Gos, if possible, and Rinkitink had no desire to remain in Regos.

Buzzub and the warriors stood silently on the shore and watched the black boat with its silver lining depart, and I am sure they were as glad to be rid of their unwelcome visitors as Inga and Rinkitink and Bilbil were to leave.

The boy asked the White Pearl what direction the boat of King Gos had taken and then he

followed after it, rowing hard and steadily for eight days without becoming at all weary. But, although the black boat moved very swiftly, it failed to overtake the barge which was rowed by Queen Cor's forty picked oarsmen.

The Nome King

CHAPTER 17

THE Kingdom of the
Nomes does not border
on the Nonestic Ocean,
from which it is sepa-
rated by the Kingdom of
Rinkitink and the Country of the Wheelers,
which is a part of the Land of Ev. Rinkitink's
country is separated from the country of the
Nomes by a row of high and steep mountains,
from which it extends to the sea. The Country
of the Wheelers is a sandy waste that is open
on one side to the Nonestic Ocean and on the
other side has no barrier to separate it from the
Nome Country, therefore it was on the coast of
the Wheelers that King Gos landed—in a spot
quite deserted by any of the curious inhabitants
of that country.

The Nome Country is very large in extent, and is only separated from the Land of Oz, on its eastern borders, by a Deadly Desert that cannot be crossed by mortals, unless they are aided by the fairies or by magic.

The nomes are a numerous and mischievous people, living in underground caverns of wide extent, connected one with another by arches and passages. The word "nome" means "one who knows," and these people are so called because they know where all the gold and silver and precious stones are hidden in the earth—a knowledge that no other living creatures share with them. The nomes are busy people, constantly digging up gold in one place and taking it to another place, where they secretly bury it, and perhaps this is the reason they alone know where to find it. The nomes were ruled, at the time of which I write, by a King named Kaliko.

King Gos had expected to be pursued by Inga in his magic boat, so he made all the haste possible, urging his forty rowers to their best efforts night and day. To his joy he was not overtaken but landed on the sandy beach of the Wheelers on the morning of the eighth day.

The forty rowers were left with the boat, while Queen Cor and King Gos, with their royal prisoners, who were still chained, began the journey to the Nome King.

It was not long before they passed the sands

and reached the rocky country belonging to the nomes, but they were still a long way from the entrance to the underground caverns in which lived the Nome King. There was a dim path, winding between stones and boulders, over which the walking was quite difficult, especially as the path led up hills that were small mountains, and then down steep and abrupt slopes where any misstep might mean a broken leg. Therefore it was the second day of their journey before they climbed halfway up a rugged mountain and found themselves at the entrance of the Nome King's caverns.

On their arrival, the entrance seemed free and unguarded, but Gos and Cor had been there before, and they were too wise to attempt to enter without announcing themselves, for the passage to the caves was full of traps and pitfalls. So King Gos stood still and shouted, and in an instant they were surrounded by a group of crooked nomes, who seemed to have sprung from the ground.

One of these had very long ears and was called The Long-Eared Hearer. He said: "I heard you coming early this morning."

Another had eyes that looked in different directions at the same time and were curiously bright and penetrating. He could look over a hill or around a corner and was called The Lookout. Said he: "I saw you coming yesterday."

"Then," said King Gos, "perhaps King Kaliko is expecting us."

"It is true," replied another nome, who wore a gold collar around his neck and carried a bunch of golden keys. "The mighty Nome King expects you, and bids you follow me to his presence."

With this he led the way into the caverns and Gos and Cor followed, dragging their weary prisoners with them, for poor King Kitticut and his gentle Queen had been obliged to carry, all through the tedious journey, the bags of gold and jewels which were to bribe the Nome King to accept them as slaves.

Through several long passages the guide led them and at last they entered a small cavern which was beautifully decorated and set with rare jewels that flashed from every part of the wall, floor and ceiling. This was a waiting-room for visitors, and there their guide left them while he went to inform King Kaliko of their arrival.

Before long they were ushered into a great domed chamber, cut from the solid rock and so magnificent that all of them—the King and Queen of Pingaree and the King and Queen of Regos and Coregos—drew long breaths of astonishment and opened their eyes as wide as they could.

In an ivory throne sat a little round man who had a pointed beard and hair that rose to a tall curl on top of his head. He was dressed in silken robes, richly embroidered, which had large buttons of cut rubies. On his head was a diamond crown and in his hand he held a golden sceptre with a big jeweled ball at one end of it. This was Kaliko, the King and ruler of all the nomes. He nodded pleasantly enough to his visitors and said in a cheery voice:

"Well, Your Majesties, what can I do for you?"

"It is my desire," answered King Gos, respectfully, "to place in your care two prisoners, whom you now see before you. They must be carefully guarded, to prevent them from escaping, for they have the cunning of foxes and are not to be trusted. In return for the favor I am asking you to grant, I have brought Your Majesty valuable presents of gold and precious gems."

He then commanded Kitticut and Garee to lay before the Nome King the bags of gold and jewels, and they obeyed, being helpless.

"Very good," said King Kaliko, nodding approval, for like all the nomes he loved treasures of gold and jewels. "But who are the prisoners you have brought here, and why do you place them in my charge instead of guarding them yourself? They seem gentle enough, I'm sure."

"The prisoners," returned King Gos, "are the King and Queen of Pingaree, a small island north of here. They are very evil people and came to our islands of Regos and Coregos to conquer them and slay our poor people. Also they intended to plunder us of all our riches, but by good fortune we were able to defeat and capture them. However, they have a son who is a terrible wizard and who by magic art is trying to find this awful King and Queen of Pingaree, and to set them free, that they may continue their wicked deeds. Therefore, as we have no magic to defend ourselves with, we have brought the prisoners to you for safe keeping."

"Your Majesty," spoke up King Kitticut, addressing the Nome King with great indignation, "do not believe this tale, I implore you. It is all a lie!"

"I know it," said Kaliko. "I consider it a clever lie, though, because it is woven without a thread of truth. However, that is none of my business. The fact remains that my good friend King Gos wishes to put you in my underground caverns, so that you will be unable to escape. And why should I not please him in this little matter? Gos is a mighty King and a great warrior, while your island of Pingaree is desolated and your people scattered. In my heart, King Kitticut, I sympathize with you, but as a matter of business policy we powerful Kings must stand together and trample the weaker ones under our feet."

King Kitticut was surprised to find the King of the nomes so candid and so well informed, and he tried to argue that he and his gentle wife did not deserve their cruel fate and that it would be wiser for Kaliko to side with them than with the evil King of Regos. But Kaliko only shook his head and smiled, saying:

"The fact that you are a prisoner, my poor Kitticut, is evidence that you are weaker than King Gos, and I prefer to deal with the strong. By the way," he added, turning to the King of Regos, "have these prisoners any connection with the Land of Oz?"

"Why do you ask?" said Gos.

"Because I dare not offend the Oz people," was the reply. "I am very powerful, as you know, but Ozma of Oz is far more powerful than I; therefore, if this King and Queen of Pingaree happened to be under Ozma's protection, I would have nothing to do with them."

"I assure Your Majesty that the prisoners have nothing to do with the Oz people," Gos hastened to say. And Kitticut, being questioned, admitted that this was true.

"But how about that wizard you mentioned?" asked the Nome King.

"Oh, he is merely a boy; but he is very ferocious and obstinate and he is assisted by a little fat sorcerer called Kinkitink and a talking goat."

"Oho! A talking goat, do you say? That cer-

tainly sounds like magic; and it also sounds like
the Land of Oz, where all the animals talk,"
said Kaliko, with a doubtful expression.

But King Gos assured him the talking goat
had never been to Oz.

"As for Rinkitink, whom you call a sorcerer,"
continued the Nome King, "he is a neighbor of
mine, you must know, but as we are cut off from
each other by high mountains beneath which a
powerful river runs, I have never yet met King
Rinkitink. But I have heard of him, and from
all reports he is a jolly rogue, and perfectly harmless. However, in spite of your false statements
and misrepresentations, I will earn the treasure
you have brought me, by keeping your prisoners
safe in my caverns."

"Make them work," advised Queen Cor.
"They are rather delicate, and to make them
work will make them suffer delightfully."

"I'll do as I please about that," said the Nome
King sternly. "Be content that I agree to keep
them safe."

The bargain being thus made and concluded,
Kaliko first examined the gold and jewels and
then sent it away to his royal storehouse, which
was well filled with like treasure. Next the captives were sent away in charge of the nome with
the golden collar and keys, whose name was Klik,
and he escorted them to a small cavern and gave
them a good supper.

"I shall lock your door," said Klik, "so there is no need of your wearing those heavy chains any longer." He therefore removed the chains and left King Kitticut and his Queen alone. This was the first time since the Northmen had carried them away from Pingaree that the good King and Queen had been alone together and free of all bonds, and as they embraced lovingly and mingled their tears over their sad fate they were also grateful that they had passed from the control of the heartless King Gos into the more considerate care of King Kaliko. They were still captives but they believed they would be happier in the underground caverns of the nomes than in Regos and Coregos.

Meantime, in the King's royal cavern a great feast had been spread. King Gos and Queen Cor, having triumphed in their plot, were so well pleased that they held high revelry with the jolly Nome King until a late hour that night. And the next morning, having cautioned Kaliko not to release the prisoners under any consideration without their orders, the King and Queen of Regos and Coregos left the caverns of the nomes to return to the shore of the ocean where they had left their boat.

Inga Parts With His Pink Pearl

CHAPTER 18

THE White Pearl guided Inga truly in his pursuit of the boat of King Gos, but the boy had been so delayed in sending his people home to Pingaree that it was a full day after Gos and Cor landed on the shore of the Wheeler Country that Inga's boat arrived at the same place.

There he found the forty rowers guarding the barge of Queen Cor, and although they would not or could not tell the boy where the King and Queen had taken his father and mother, the White Pearl advised him to follow the path to the country and the caverns of the nomes.

Rinkitink didn't like to undertake the rocky and mountainous journey, even with Bilbil to carry him, but he would not desert Inga, even though his own kingdom lay just beyond a range of mountains which could be seen towering southwest of them. So the King bravely mounted the goat, who always grumbled but always obeyed his master, and the three set off at once for the caverns of the nomes.

They traveled just as slowly as Queen Cor and King Gos had done, so when they were about halfway they discovered the King and Queen coming back to their boat. The fact that Gos and Cor were now alone proved that they had left Inga's father and mother behind them; so, at the suggestion of Rinkitink, the three hid behind a high rock until the King of Regos and the Queen of Coregos, who had not observed them, had passed them by. Then they continued their journey, glad that they had not again been forced to fight or quarrel with their wicked enemies.

"We might have asked them, however, what they had done with your poor parents," said Rinkitink.

"Never mind," answered Inga. "I am sure the White Pearl will guide us aright."

For a time they proceeded in silence and then Rinkitink began to chuckle with laughter in the pleasant way he was wont to do before his misfortunes came upon him.

"What amuses Your Majesty?" inquired the boy.

"The thought of how surprised my dear subjects would be if they realized how near to them I am, and yet how far away. I have always wanted to visit the Nome Country, which is full of mystery and magic and all sorts of adventures, but my devoted subjects forbade me to think of such a thing, fearing I would get hurt or enchanted."

"Are you afraid, now that you are here?" asked Inga.

"A little, but not much, for they say the new Nome King is not as wicked as the old King used to be. Still, we are undertaking a dangerous journey and I think you ought to protect me by lending me one of your pearls."

Inga thought this over and it seemed a reasonable request.

"Which pearl would you like to have?" asked the boy.

"Well, let us see," returned Rinkitink; "you may need strength to liberate your captive parents, so you must keep the Blue Pearl. And you will need the advice of the White Pearl, so you had best keep that also. But in case we should be separated I would have nothing to protect me from harm, so you ought to lend me the Pink Pearl."

"Very well," agreed Inga, and sitting down upon a rock he removed his right shoe and after withdrawing the cloth from the pointed toe took out the Pink Pearl—the one which protected from any harm the person who carried it.

"Where can you put it, to keep it safely?" he asked.

"In my vest pocket," replied the King. "The pocket has a flap to it and I can pin it down in such a way that the pearl cannot get out and become lost. As for robbery, no one with evil intent can touch my person while I have the pearl."

So Inga gave Rinkitink the Pink Pearl and the little King placed it in the pocket of his red-and-green brocaded velvet vest, pinning the flap of the pocket down tightly.

They now resumed their journey and finally reached the entrance to the Nome King's caverns. Placing the White Pearl to his ear, Inga asked: "What shall I do now?" and the Voice of the Pearl replied: "Clap your hands together four times and call aloud the word 'Klik.' Then allow yourselves to be conducted to the Nome King, who is now holding your father and mother captive."

Inga followed these instructions and when Klik appeared in answer to his summons the boy requested an audience of the Nome King. So Klik led them into the presence of King Kaliko, who was suffering from a severe headache, due to his revelry the night before, and therefore was unusually cross and grumpy.

"I know what you've come for," said he, be-

fore Inga could speak. "You want to get the captives from Regos away from me; but you can't do it, so you'd best go away again."

"The captives are my father and mother, and I intend to liberate them," said the boy firmly.

The King stared hard at Inga, wondering at his audacity. Then he turned to look at King Rinkitink and said:

"I suppose you are the King of Gilgad, which is in the Kingdom of Rinkitink."

"You've guessed it the first time," replied Rinkitink.

"How round and fat you are!" exclaimed Kaliko.

"I was just thinking how fat and round *you* are," said Rinkitink. "Really, King Kaliko, we ought to be friends, we're so much alike in everything but disposition and intelligence."

Then he began to chuckle, while Kaliko stared hard at him, not knowing whether to accept his speech as a compliment or not. And now the nome's eyes wandered to Bilbil, and he asked:

"Is that your talking goat?"

Bilbil met the Nome King's glowering look with a gaze equally surly and defiant, while Rinkitink answered: "It is, Your Majesty."

"Can he really talk?" asked Kaliko, curiously.

"He can. But the best thing he does is to scold. Talk to His Majesty, Bilbil."

But Bilbil remained silent and would not speak.

"Do you always ride upon his back?" continued Kaliko, questioning Rinkitink.

"Yes," was the answer, "because it is difficult for a fat man to walk far, as perhaps you know from experience."

"That is true," said Kaliko. "Get off the goat's back and let me ride him a while, to see how I like it. Perhaps I'll take him away from you, to ride through my caverns."

Rinkitink chuckled softly as he heard this, but at once got off Bilbil's back and let Kaliko get on. The Nome King was a little awkward, but when he was firmly astride the saddle he called in a loud voice: "Giddap!"

When Bilbil paid no attention to the command and refused to stir, Kaliko kicked his heels viciously against the goat's body, and then Bilbil made a sudden start. He ran swiftly across the great cavern, until he had almost reached the opposite wall, when he stopped so abruptly that King Kaliko sailed over his head and bumped against the jeweled wall. He bumped so hard that the points of his crown were all mashed out of shape and his head was driven far into the diamond-studded band of the crown, so that it covered one eye and a part of his nose. Perhaps this saved Kaliko's head from being cracked

against the rock wall, but it was hard on the crown.

Bilbil was highly pleased at the success of his feat and Rinkitink laughed merrily at the Nome King's comical appearance; but Kaliko was muttering and growling as he picked himself up and struggled to pull the battered crown from his head, and it was evident that he was not in the least amused. Indeed, Inga could see that the King was very angry, and the boy knew that the incident was likely to turn Kaliko against the entire party.

The Nome King sent Klik for another crown and ordered his workmen to repair the one that was damaged. While he waited for the new crown he sat regarding his visitors with a scowling face, and this made Inga more uneasy than ever. Finally, when the new crown was placed upon his head, King Kaliko said: "Follow me, strangers!" and led the way to a small door at one end of the cavern.

Inga and Rinkitink followed him through the doorway and found themselves standing on a balcony that overlooked an enormous domed cave—so extensive that it seemed miles to the other side of it. All around this circular cave, which was brilliantly lighted from an unknown source, were arches connected with other caverns.

Kaliko took a gold whistle from his pocket and

blew a shrill note that echoed through every part of the cave. Instantly nomes began to pour in through the side arches in great numbers, until the immense space was packed with them as far as the eye could reach. All were armed with glittering weapons of polished silver and gold, and Inga was amazed that any King could command so great an army.

They began marching and countermarching in very orderly array until another blast of the gold whistle sent them scurrying away as quickly as they had appeared. And as soon as the great cave was again empty Kaliko returned with his visitors to his own royal chamber, where he once more seated himself upon his ivory throne.

"I have shown you," said he to Inga, "a part of my bodyguard. The royal armies, of which this is only a part, are as numerous as the sands of the ocean, and live in many thousands of my underground caverns. You have come here thinking to force me to give up the captives of King Gos and Queen Cor, and I wanted to convince you that my power is too mighty for anyone to oppose. I am told that you are a wizard, and depend upon magic to aid you; but you must know that the nomes are not mortals, and understand magic pretty well themselves, so if we are obliged to fight magic with magic the chances are that we are a hundred times more powerful than you can be. Think this over carefully, my boy, and try to realize that you are in my power. I do not believe you can force me to liberate King Kitticut and Queen Garee, and I know that you cannot coax me to do so, for I have given my promise to King Gos. Therefore, as I do not wish to hurt you, I ask you to go away peaceably and let me alone."

"Forgive me if I do not agree with you, King Kaliko," answered the boy. "However difficult and dangerous my task may be, I cannot leave your dominions until every effort to release my parents has failed and left me completely discouraged."

"Very well," said the King, evidently displeased. "I have warned you, and now if evil overtakes you it is your own fault. I've a headache to-day, so I cannot entertain you properly, according to your rank; but Klik will attend you to my guest chambers and to-morrow I will talk with you again."

This seemed a fair and courteous way to treat one's declared enemies, so they politely expressed the wish that Kaliko's headache would be better, and followed their guide, Klik, down a well-lighted passage and through several archways until they finally reached three nicely furnished bedchambers which were cut from solid gray rock and well lighted and aired by some mysterious method known to the nomes.

The first of these rooms was given King Rinkitink, the second was Inga's and the third was assigned to Bilbil the goat. There was a swinging rock door between the third and second rooms and another between the second and first, which also had a door that opened upon the passage. Rinkitink's room was the largest, so it was here that an excellent dinner was spread by some of the nome servants, who, in spite of their crooked shapes, proved to be well trained and competent.

"You are not prisoners, you know," said Klik; "neither are you welcome guests, having declared your purpose to oppose our mighty King and all his hosts. But we bear you no ill will, and you are to be well fed and cared for as long as you remain in our caverns. Eat hearty, sleep tight, and pleasant dreams to you."

Saying this, he left them alone and at once Rinkitink and Inga began to counsel together as to the best means to liberate King Kitticut and Queen Garee. The White Pearl's advice was rather unsatisfactory to the boy, just now, for all that the Voice said in answer to his questions was: "Be patient, brave and determined."

Rinkitink suggested that they try to discover in what part of the series of underground caverns Inga's parents had been confined, as that knowledge was necessary before they could take any action; so together they started out, leaving Bilbil asleep in his room, and made their way unopposed through many corridors and caverns.

In some places were great furnaces, where gold dust was being melted into bricks. In other rooms workmen were fashioning the gold into various articles and ornaments. In one cavern immense wheels revolved which polished precious gems, and they found many caverns used as storerooms, where treasure of every sort was piled high. Also they came to the barracks of the army and the great kitchens.

There were nomes everywhere—countless thousands of them—but none paid the slightest heed to the visitors from the earth's surface. Yet, although Inga and Rinkitink walked until they were weary, they were unable to locate the place where the boy's father and mother had been confined, and when they tried to return to their own rooms they found that they had hopelessly lost themselves amid the labyrinth of passages. However, Klik presently came to them, laughing at their discomfiture, and led them back to their bedchambers.

Before they went to sleep they carefully barred the door from Rinkitink's room to the corridor, but the doors that connected the three rooms one with another were left wide open.

In the night Inga was awakened by a soft grating sound that filled him with anxiety because he could not account for it. It was dark in his room, the light having disappeared as soon as he got into bed, but he managed to feel his way to the door that led to Rinkitink's room and found it tightly closed and immovable. Then he made his way to the opposite door, leading to Bilbil's room, to discover that also had been closed and fastened.

The boy had a curious sensation that all of his room—the walls, floor and ceiling—was slowly whirling as if on a pivot, and it was such an uncomfortable feeling that he got into bed again, not knowing what else to do. And as the grating noise had ceased and the room now seemed stationary, he soon fell asleep again.

When the boy wakened, after many hours, he found the room again light. So he dressed himself and discovered that a small table, containing a breakfast that was smoking hot, had suddenly appeared in the center of his room. He tried the two doors, but finding that he could not open them he ate some breakfast, thoughtfully wondering who had locked him in and why he had been made a prisoner. Then he again went to the door which he thought led to Rinkitink's chamber and to his surprise the latch lifted easily and the door swung open.

Before him was a rude corridor hewn in the rock and dimly lighted. It did not look inviting, so Inga closed the door, puzzled to know what had become of Rinkitink's room and the King, and went to the opposite door. Opening this, he

found a solid wall of rock confronting him, which effectually prevented his escape in that direction.

The boy now realized that King Kaliko had tricked him, and while professing to receive him as a guest had plotted to separate him from his comrades. One way had been left, however, by which he might escape and he decided to see where it led to.

So, going to the first door, he opened it and ventured slowly into the dimly lighted corridor. When he had advanced a few steps he heard the door of his room slam shut behind him. He ran back at once, but the door of rock fitted so closely into the wall that he found it impossible to open it again. That did not matter so much, however, for the room was a prison and the only way of escape seemed ahead of him.

Along the corridor he crept until, turning a corner, he found himself in a large domed cavern that was empty and deserted. Here also was a dim light that permitted him to see another corridor at the opposite side; so he crossed the rocky floor of the cavern and entered a second corridor. This one twisted and turned in every direction but was not very long, so soon the boy reached a second cavern, not so large as the first. This he found vacant also, but it had another corridor leading out of it, so Inga entered that. It was straight and short and beyond was a third cavern, which differed little from the others except that it had a strong iron grating at one side of it.

All three of these caverns had been roughly hewn from the rock and it seemed they had never been put to use, as had all the other caverns of the nomes he had visited. Standing in the third cavern, Inga saw what he thought was still another corridor at its farther side, so he walked toward it. This opening was dark, and that fact, and the solemn silence all around him, made him hesitate for a while to enter it. Upon reflection, however, he realized that unless he explored the place to the very end he could not hope to escape from it, so he boldly entered the dark corridor and felt his way cautiously as he moved forward.

Scarcely had he taken two paces when a crash resounded back of him and a heavy sheet of steel closed the opening into the cavern from which he had just come. He paused a moment, but it still seemed best to proceed, and as Inga advanced in the dark, holding his hands outstretched before him to feel his way, handcuffs fell upon his wrists and locked themselves with a sharp click, and an instant later he found he was chained to a stout iron post set firmly in the rock floor.

The chains were long enough to permit him to move a yard or so in any direction and by feeling the walls he found he was in a small circular room that had no outlet except the passage by which he had entered, and that was now closed by the door of steel. This was the end of the series of caverns and corridors.

It was now that the horror of his situation occurred to the boy with full force. But he resolved not to submit to his fate without a struggle, and realizing that he possessed the Blue Pearl, which gave him marvelous strength, he quickly broke the chains and set himself free of the handcuffs. Next he twisted the steel door from its hinges, and creeping along the short passage, found himself in the third cave.

But now the dim light, which had before guided him, had vanished; yet on peering into the gloom of the cave he saw what appeared to be two round disks of flame, which cast a subdued glow over the floor and walls. By this dull glow he made out the form of an enormous man, seated in the center of the cave, and he saw that the iron grating had been removed, permitting the man to enter.

The giant was unclothed and its limbs were thickly covered with coarse red hair. The round disks of flame were its two eyes and when it opened its mouth to yawn Inga saw that its jaws were wide enough to crush a dozen men between the great rows of teeth.

Presently the giant looked up and perceived

the boy crouching at the other side of the cavern, so he called out in a hoarse, rude voice:

"Come hither, my pretty one. We will wrestle together, you and I, and if you succeed in throwing me I will let you pass through my cave."

The boy made no reply to the challenge. He realized he was in dire peril and regretted that he had lent the Pink Pearl to King Rinkitink. But it was now too late for vain regrets, although he feared that even his great strength would avail him little against this hairy monster. For his arms were not long enough to span a fourth of the giant's huge body, while the monster's powerful limbs would be likely to crush out Inga's life before he could gain the mastery.

Therefore the Prince resolved to employ other means to combat this foe, who had doubtless been placed there to bar his return. Retreating through the passage he reached the room where he had been chained and wrenched the iron post from its socket. It was a foot thick and four feet long, and being of solid iron was so heavy that three ordinary men would have found it hard to lift.

Returning to the cavern, the boy swung the great bar above his head and dashed it with mighty force full at the giant. The end of the bar struck the monster upon its forehead, and with a single groan it fell full length upon the floor and lay still.

When the giant fell, the glow from its eyes faded away, and all was dark. Cautiously, for Inga was not sure the giant was dead, the boy felt his way toward the opening that led to the middle cavern. The entrance was narrow and the darkness was intense, but, feeling braver now, the boy stepped boldly forward. Instantly the floor began to sink beneath him and in great alarm he turned and made a leap that enabled him to grasp the rocky sides of the wall and regain a footing in the passage through which he had just come.

Scarcely had he obtained this place of refuge when a mighty crash resounded throughout the cavern and the sound of a rushing torrent came from far below. Inga felt in his pocket and found several matches, one of which he lighted and held before him. While it flickered he saw that the entire floor of the cavern had fallen away, and knew that had he not instantly regained his footing in the passage he would have plunged into the abyss that lay beneath him.

By the light of another match he saw the opening at the other side of the cave and the thought came to him that possibly he might leap across the gulf. Of course, this could never be accomplished without the marvelous strength lent him by the Blue Pearl, but Inga had the feeling that one powerful spring might carry him over the chasm into safety. He could not

stay where he was, that was certain, so he resolved to make the attempt.

He took a long run through the first cave and the short corridor; then, exerting all his strength, he launched himself over the black gulf of the second cave. Swiftly he flew and, although his heart stood still with fear, only a few seconds elapsed before his feet touched the ledge of the opposite passageway and he knew he had safely accomplished the wonderful feat.

Only pausing to draw one long breath of relief, Inga quickly traversed the crooked corridor that led to the last cavern of the three. But when he came in sight of it he paused abruptly, his eyes nearly blinded by a glare of strong light which burst upon them. Covering his face with his hands, Inga retreated behind a projecting corner of rock and by gradually getting his eyes used to the light he was finally able to gaze without blinking upon the strange glare that had so quickly changed the condition of the cavern. When he had passed through this vault it had been entirely empty. Now the flat floor of rock was covered everywhere with a bed of glowing coals, which shot up little tongues of red and white flames. Indeed, the entire cave was one monster furnace and the heat that came from it was fearful.

Inga's heart sank within him as he realized the terrible obstacle placed by the cunning

Nome King between him and the safety of the other caverns. There was no turning back, for it would be impossible for him again to leap over the gulf of the second cave, the corridor at this side being so crooked that he could get no run before he jumped. Neither could he leap over the glowing coals of the cavern that faced him, for it was much larger than the middle cavern. In this dilemma he feared his great strength would avail him nothing and he bitterly reproached himself for parting with the Pink Pearl, which would have preserved him from injury.

However, it was not in the nature of Prince Inga to despair for long, his past adventures having taught him confidence and courage, sharpened his wits and given him the genius of invention. He sat down and thought earnestly on the means of escape from his danger and at last a clever idea came to his mind. This is the way to get ideas: never to let adverse circumstances discourage you, but to believe there is a way out of every difficulty, which may be found by earnest thought.

There were many points and projections of rock in the walls of the crooked corridor in which Inga stood and some of these rocks had become cracked and loosened, although still clinging to their places. The boy picked out one large piece, and, exerting all his strength, tore it away from the wall. He then carried it to the cavern and tossed it upon the burning coals, about ten feet away from the end of the passage. Then he returned for another fragment of rock, and wrenching it free from its place, he threw it ten feet beyond the first one, toward the opposite side of the cave. The boy continued this work until he had made a series of stepping-stones reaching straight across the cavern to the dark passageway beyond, which he hoped would lead him back to safety if not to liberty.

When his work had been completed, Inga did not long hesitate to take advantage of his stepping-stones, for he knew his best chance of escape lay in his crossing the bed of coals before the rocks became so heated that they would burn his feet. So he leaped to the first rock and from there began jumping from one to the other in quick succession. A withering wave of heat at once enveloped him, and for a time he feared he would suffocate before he could cross the cavern; but he held his breath, to keep the hot air from his lungs, and maintained his leaps with desperate resolve.

Then, before he realized it, his feet were pressing the cooler rocks of the passage beyond and he rolled helpless upon the floor, gasping for breath. His skin was so red that it resembled the shell of a boiled lobster, but his swift motion had prevented his being burned, and his shoes had thick soles, which saved his feet.

After resting a few minutes, the boy felt strong enough to go on. He went to the end of the passage and found that the rock door by which he had left his room was still closed, so he returned to about the middle of the corridor and was thinking what he should do next, when suddenly the solid rock before him began to move and an opening appeared through which shone a brilliant light. Shielding his eyes, which were somewhat dazzled, Inga sprang through the opening and found himself in one of the Nome King's inhabited caverns, where before him stood King Kaliko, with a broad grin upon his features, and Klik, the King's chamberlain, who looked surprised, and King Rinkitink seated astride Bilbil the goat, both of whom seemed pleased that Inga had rejoined them.

Rinkitink Chuckles

CHAPTER 19

WE will now relate
what happened to Rink-
itink and Bilbil that
morning, while Inga was
undergoing his trying
experience in escaping the fearful dangers of the
three caverns.

The King of Gilgad wakened to find the door
of Inga's room fast shut and locked, but he had
no trouble in opening his own door into the
corridor, for it seems that the boy's room, which
was the middle one, whirled around on a pivot,
while the adjoining rooms occupied by Bilbil and
Rinkitink remained stationary. The little King
also found a breakfast magically served in his
room, and while he was eating it, Klik came to
him and stated that His Majesty, King Kaliko,

desired his presence in the royal cavern.

So Rinkitink, having first made sure that the Pink Pearl was still in his vest pocket, willingly followed Klik, who ran on some distance ahead. But no sooner had Rinkitink set foot in the passage than a great rock, weighing at least a ton, became dislodged and dropped from the roof directly over his head. Of course, it could not harm him, protected as he was by the Pink Pearl, and it bounded aside and crashed upon the floor, where it was shattered by its own weight.

"How careless!" exclaimed the little King, and waddled after Klik, who seemed amazed at his escape.

Presently another rock above Rinkitink plunged downward, and then another, but none touched his body. Klik seemed much perplexed at these continued escapes and certainly Kaliko was surprised when Rinkitink, safe and sound, entered the royal cavern.

"Good morning," said the King of Gilgad. "Your rocks are getting loose, Kaliko, and you'd better have them glued in place before they hurt someone." Then he began to chuckle: "Hoo, hoo, hoo-hee, hee-heek, keek, eek!" and Kaliko sat and frowned because he realized that the little fat King was poking fun at him.

"I asked Your Majesty to come here," said the Nome King, "to show you a curious skein of golden thread which my workmen have made. If it pleases you, I will make you a present of it."

With this he held out a small skein of glittering gold twine, which was really pretty and curious. Rinkitink took it in his hand and at once the golden thread began to unwind—so swiftly that the eye could not follow its motion. And, as it unwound, it coiled itself around Rinkitink's body, at the same time weaving itself into a net, until it had enveloped the little King from head to foot and placed him in a prison of gold.

"Aha!" cried Kaliko; "*this* magic worked all right, it seems."

"Oh, did it?" replied Rinkitink, and stepping forward he walked right through the golden net, which fell to the floor in a tangled mass.

Kaliko rubbed his chin thoughtfully and stared hard at Rinkitink.

"I understand a good bit of magic," said he, "but Your Majesty has a sort of magic that greatly puzzles me, because it is unlike anything of the sort that I ever met with before."

"Now, see here, Kaliko," said Rinkitink; "if you are trying to harm me or my companions, give it up, for you will never succeed. We're harm-proof, so to speak, and you are merely wasting your time trying to injure us."

"You may be right, and I hope I am not so impolite as to argue with a guest," returned the Nome King. "But you will pardon me if I am not yet satisfied that you are stronger than my famous magic. However, I beg you to believe that I bear you no ill will, King Rinkitink; but it is my duty to destroy you, if possible, because you and that insignificant boy Prince have openly threatened to take away my captives and have positively refused to go back to the earth's surface and let me alone. I'm very tender-hearted, as a matter of fact, and I like you immensely and would enjoy having you as a friend, but—" Here he pressed a button on the arm of his throne chair and the section of the floor where Rinkitink stood suddenly opened and disclosed a black pit beneath, which was a part of the terrible Bottomless Gulf.

But Rinkitink did not fall into the pit; his body remained suspended in the air until he put out his foot and stepped to the solid floor, when the opening suddenly closed again.

"I appreciate Your Majesty's friendship," remarked Rinkitink, as calmly as if nothing had happened, "but I am getting tired with standing. Will you kindly send for my goat, Bilbil, that I may sit upon his back to rest?"

"Indeed I will!" promised Kaliko. "I have not yet completed my test of your magic, and as I owe that goat a slight grudge for bumping my head and smashing my second-best crown, I will be glad to discover if the beast can also escape my delightful little sorceries."

So Klik was sent to fetch Bilbil and presently returned with the goat, which was very cross this morning because it had not slept well in the underground caverns.

Rinkitink lost no time in getting upon the red velvet saddle which the goat constantly wore, for he feared the Nome King would try to destroy Bilbil and knew that as long as his body touched that of the goat the Pink Pearl would protect them both; whereas, if Bilbil stood alone, there was no magic to save him.

Bilbil glared wickedly at King Kaliko, who moved uneasily in his ivory throne. Then the Nome King whispered a moment in the ear of Klik, who nodded and left the room.

"Please make yourselves at home here for a few minutes, while I attend to an errand," said the Nome King, getting up from the throne. "I shall return pretty soon, when I hope to find you pieceful—ha, ha, ha!—that's a joke you can't appreciate now but will later. Be pieceful—that's the idea. Ho, ho, ho! How funny." Then he waddled from the cavern, closing the door behind him.

"Well, why didn't you laugh when Kaliko laughed?" demanded the goat, when they were left alone in the cavern.

"Because he means mischief of some sort," replied Rinkitink, "and we'll laugh after the danger is over, Bilbil. There's an old adage that says: 'He laughs best who laughs last,' and the only way to laugh last is to give the other fellow a chance. Where did that knife come from, I wonder."

For a long, sharp knife suddenly appeared in the air near them, twisting and turning from side to side and darting here and there in a dangerous manner, without any support whatever. Then another knife became visible—and another and another—until all the space in the royal cavern seemed filled with them. Their sharp points and edges darted toward Rinkitink and Bilbil perpetually and nothing could have saved them from being cut to pieces except the protecting power of the Pink Pearl. As it was, not a knife touched them and even Bilbil gave a gruff laugh at the failure of Kaliko's clever magic.

The goat wandered here and there in the cavern, carrying Rinkitink upon his back, and neither of them paid the slightest heed to the knives, although the glitter of the hundreds of polished blades was rather trying to their eyes. Perhaps for ten minutes the knives darted about them in bewildering fury; then they disappeared as suddenly as they had appeared.

Kaliko cautiously stuck his head through the doorway and found the goat chewing the embroidery of his royal cloak, which he had left lying over the throne, while Rinkitink was reading his manuscript on "How to be Good" and chuckling over its advice. The Nome King seemed greatly disappointed as he came in and resumed his seat on the throne. Said Rinkitink with a chuckle:

"We've really had a peaceful time, Kaliko, although not the pieceful time you expected. Forgive me if I indulge in a laugh—hoo, hoo, hoohee, heek-keek-eek! And now, tell me; aren't you getting tired of trying to injure us?"

"Eh-heh," said the Nome King. "I see now that your magic can protect you from all my arts. But is the boy Inga as well protected as Your Majesty and the goat?"

"Why do you ask?" inquired Rinkitink, uneasy at the question because he remembered he had not seen the little Prince of Pingaree that morning.

"Because," said Kaliko, "the boy has been undergoing trials far greater and more dangerous than any you have encountered, and it has been hundreds of years since anyone has been able to escape alive from the perils of my Three Trick Caverns."

King Rinkitink was much alarmed at hearing this, for although he knew that Inga possessed the Blue Pearl, that would only give to him marvelous strength, and perhaps strength alone would not enable him to escape from danger. But he would not let Kaliko see the fear he felt for Inga's safety, so he said in a careless way:

"You're a mighty poor magician, Kaliko, and I'll give you my crown if Inga hasn't escaped any danger you have threatened him with."

"Your whole crown is not worth one of the valuable diamonds in my crown," answered the Nome King, "but I'll take it. Let us go at once, therefore, and see what has become of the boy Prince, for if he is not destroyed by this time I will admit he cannot be injured by any of the magic arts which I have at my command."

He left the room, accompanied by Klik, who had now rejoined his master, and by Rinkitink riding upon Bilbil. After traversing several of the huge caverns they entered one that was somewhat more bright and cheerful than the others, where the Nome King paused before a wall of rock. Then Klik pressed a secret spring and a section of the wall opened and disclosed the corridor where Prince Inga stood facing them.

"Tarts and tadpoles!" cried Kaliko in surprise. "The boy is still alive!"

Dorothy to the Rescue

CHAPTER 20

ONE day when Princess Dorothy of Oz was visiting Glinda the Good, who is Ozma's Royal Sorceress, she was looking through Glinda's Great Book of Records —wherein is inscribed all important events that happen in every part of the world—when she came upon the record of the destruction of Pingaree, the capture of King Kitticut and Queen Garee and all their people, and the curious escape of Inga, the boy Prince, and of King Rinkitink and the talking goat. Turning over some of the following pages, Dorothy read how Inga had found the Magic Pearls and was rowing the silver-lined boat to Regos to try to rescue his parents.

The little girl was much interested to know how well Inga succeeded, but she returned to the palace of Ozma at the Emerald City of Oz the next day and other events made her forget the boy Prince of Pingaree for a time. However, she was one day idly looking at Ozma's Magic Picture, which shows any scene you may wish to see, when the girl thought of Inga and commanded the Magic Picture to show what the boy was doing at that moment.

It was the time when Inga and Rinkitink had followed the King of Regos and Queen of Coregos to the Nome King's country and she saw them hiding behind the rock as Cor and Gos passed them by after having placed the King and Queen of Pingaree in the keeping of the Nome King. From that time Dorothy followed, by means of the Magic Picture, the adventures of Inga and his friend in the Nome King's caverns, and the danger and helplessness of the poor boy aroused the little girl's pity and indignation.

So she went to Ozma and told the lovely girl Ruler of Oz all about Inga and Rinkitink.

"I think Kaliko is treating them dreadfully mean," declared Dorothy, "and I wish you'd let me go to the Nome Country and help them out of their troubles."

"Go, my dear, if you wish to," replied Ozma, "but I think it would be best for you to take the Wizard with you."

"Oh, I'm not afraid of the nomes," said Dorothy, "but I'll be glad to take the Wizard, for company. And may we use your Magic Carpet, Ozma?"

"Of course. Put the Magic Carpet in the Red Wagon and have the Sawhorse take you and the Wizard to the edge of the desert. While you are gone, Dorothy, I'll watch you in the Magic Picture, and if any danger threatens you I'll see you are not harmed."

Dorothy thanked the Ruler of Oz and kissed her good-bye, for she was determined to start at once. She found the Wizard of Oz, who was planting shoetrees in the garden, and when she told him Inga's story he willingly agreed to accompany the little girl to the Nome King's caverns. They had both been there before and had conquered the nomes with ease, so they were not at all afraid.

The Wizard, who was a cheery little man with a bald head and a winning smile, harnessed the Wooden Sawhorse to the Red Wagon and loaded on Ozma's Magic Carpet. Then he and Dorothy climbed to the seat and the Sawhorse started off and carried them swiftly through the beautiful Land of Oz to the edge of the Deadly Desert that separated their fairyland from the Nome Country.

Even Dorothy and the clever Wizard would not have dared to cross this desert without the

aid of the Magic Carpet, for it would have quickly destroyed them; but when the roll of carpet had been placed upon the edge of the sands, leaving just enough lying flat for them to stand upon, the carpet straightway began to unroll before them and as they walked on it continued to unroll, until they had safely passed over the stretch of Deadly Desert and were on the border of the Nome King's dominions.

This journey had been accomplished in a few minutes, although such a distance would have required several days' travel had they not been walking on the Magic Carpet. On arriving they at once walked toward the entrance to the caverns of the nomes.

The Wizard carried a little black bag containing his tools of wizardry, while Dorothy carried over her arm a covered basket in which she had placed a dozen eggs, with which to conquer the nomes if she had any trouble with them.

Eggs may seem to you to be a queer weapon with which to fight, but the little girl well knew their value. The nomes are immortal; that is, they do not perish, as mortals do, *unless they happen to come in contact with an egg.* If an egg touches them—either the outer shell or the inside of the egg—the nomes lose their charm of perpetual life and thereafter are liable to die through accident or old age, just as all humans are.

For this reason the sight of an egg fills a nome with terror and he will do anything to prevent an egg from touching him, even for an instant. So, when Dorothy took her basket of eggs with her, she knew that she was more powerfully armed than if she had a regiment of soldiers at her back.

The Wizard Finds an Enchantment

CHAPTER 21

AFTER Kaliko had failed in his attempts to destroy his guests, as has been related, the Nome King did nothing more to injure them but treated them in a friendly manner. He refused, however, to permit Inga to see or to speak with his father and mother, or even to know in what part of the underground caverns they were confined.

"You are able to protect your lives and persons, I freely admit," said Kaliko; "but I firmly believe you have no power, either of magic or otherwise, to take from me the captives I have agreed to keep for King Gos."

Inga would not agree to this. He determined not to leave the caverns until he had liberated his father and mother, although he did not then know how that could be accomplished. As for Rinkitink, the jolly King was well fed and had a good bed to sleep upon, so he was not worrying about anything and seemed in no hurry to go away.

Kaliko and Rinkitink were engaged in pitching a game with solid gold quoits, on the floor of the royal chamber, and Inga and Bilbil were watching them, when Klik came running in, his hair standing on end with excitement, and cried out that the Wizard of Oz and Dorothy were approaching.

Kaliko turned pale on hearing this unwelcome news and, abandoning his game, went to sit in his ivory throne and try to think what had brought these fearful visitors to his domain.

"Who is Dorothy?" asked Inga.

"She is a little girl who once lived in Kansas," replied Klik, with a shudder, "but she now lives in Ozma's palace at the Emerald City and is a Princess of Oz—which means that she is a terrible foe to deal with."

"Doesn't she like the nomes?" inquired the boy.

"It isn't that," said King Kaliko, with a groan, "but she insists on the nomes being goody-goody, which is contrary to their natures. Dorothy gets angry if I do the least thing that is wicked, and tries to make me stop it, and that naturally makes me downhearted. I can't imagine why she has come here just now, for I've been behaving very well lately. As for that Wizard of Oz, he's chock-full of magic that I can't overcome, for he learned it from Glinda, who is the most powerful sorceress in the world. Woe is me! Why didn't Dorothy and the Wizard stay in Oz, where they belong?"

Inga and Rinkitink listened to this with much joy, for at once the idea came to them both to plead with Dorothy to help them. Even Bilbil pricked up his ears when he heard the Wizard of Oz mentioned, and the goat seemed much less surly, and more thoughtful than usual.

A few minutes later a nome came to say that Dorothy and the Wizard had arrived and demanded admittance, so Klik was sent to usher them into the royal presence of the Nome King.

As soon as she came in the little girl ran up to the boy Prince and seized both his hands.

"Oh, Inga!" she exclaimed, "I'm so glad to find you alive and well."

Inga was astonished at so warm a greeting. Making a low bow he said:

"I don't think we have met before, Princess."

"No, indeed," replied Dorothy, "but I know all about you and I've come to help you and King Rinkitink out of your troubles." Then she turned to the Nome King and continued: "You ought to be ashamed of yourself, King Kaliko, to treat an honest Prince and an honest King so badly."

"I haven't done anything to them," whined Kaliko, trembling as her eyes flashed upon him.

"No; but you tried to, an' that's just as bad, if not worse," said Dorothy, who was very indignant. "And now I want you to send for the King and Queen of Pingaree and have them brought here *immejitly!*"

"I won't," said Kaliko.

"Yes, you will!" cried Dorothy, stamping her foot at him. "I won't have those poor people made unhappy any longer, or separated from their little boy. Why, it's *dreadful*, Kaliko, an' I'm su'prised at you. You must be more wicked than I thought you were."

"I can't do it, Dorothy," said the Nome King, almost weeping with despair. "I promised King Gos I'd keep them captives. You wouldn't ask me to break my promise, would you?"

"King Gos was a robber and an outlaw," she said, "and p'r'aps you don't know that a storm at sea wrecked his boat, while he was going back to Regos, and that he and Queen Cor were both drowned."

"Dear me!" exclaimed Kaliko. "Is that so?"

"I saw it in Glinda's Record Book," said Dorothy. "So now you trot out the King and Queen of Pingaree as quick as you can."

"No," persisted the contrary Nome King, shaking his head, "I won't do it. Ask me any-

thing else and I'll try to please you, but I can't allow these friendly enemies to triumph over me."

"In that case," said Dorothy, beginning to remove the cover from her basket, "I'll show you some eggs."

"Eggs!" screamed the Nome King in horror. "Have you eggs in that basket?"

"A dozen of 'em," replied Dorothy.

"Then keep them there—I beg—I implore you! —and I'll do anything you say," pleaded Kaliko, his teeth chattering so that he could hardly speak.

"Send for the King and Queen of Pingaree," said Dorothy.

"Go, Klik," commanded the Nome King, and Klik ran away in great haste, for he was almost as much frightened as his master.

It was an affecting scene when the unfortunate King and Queen of Pingaree entered the chamber and with sobs and tears of joy embraced their brave and adventurous son. All the others stood silent until greetings and kisses had been exchanged and Inga had told his parents in a few words of his vain struggles to rescue them and how Princess Dorothy had finally come to his assistance.

Then King Kitticut shook the hands of his friend King Rinkitink and thanked him for so loyally supporting his son Inga, and Queen

Garee kissed little Dorothy's forehead and blessed her for restoring her husband and herself to freedom.

The Wizard had been standing near Bilbil the goat and now he was surprised to hear the animal say:

"Joyful reunion, isn't it? But it makes me tired to see grown people cry like children."

"Oho!" exclaimed the Wizard. "How does it happen, Mr. Goat, that you, who have never been to the Land of Oz, are able to talk?"

"That's my business," returned Bilbil in a surly tone.

The Wizard stooped down and gazed fixedly into the animal's eyes. Then he said, with a pitying sigh: "I see; you are under an enchantment. Indeed, I believe you to be Prince Bobo of Boboland."

Bilbil made no reply but dropped his head as if ashamed.

"This is a great discovery," said the Wizard, addressing Dorothy and the others of the party. "A good many years ago a cruel magician transformed the gallant Prince of Boboland into a talking goat, and this goat, being ashamed of his condition, ran away and was never after seen in Boboland, which is a country far to the south of here but bordering on the Deadly Desert, opposite the Land of Oz. I heard of this story long

ago and know that a diligent search has been made for the enchanted Prince, without result. But I am well assured that, in the animal you call Bilbil, I have discovered the unhappy Prince of Boboland."

"Dear me, Bilbil," said Rinkitink, "why have you never told me this?"

"What would be the use?" asked Bilbil in a low voice and still refusing to look up.

"The use?" repeated Rinkitink, puzzled.

"Yes, that's the trouble," said the Wizard. "It is one of the most powerful enchantments ever accomplished, and the magician is now dead and the secret of the anti-charm lost. Even I, with all my skill, cannot restore Prince Bobo to his proper form. But I think Glinda might be able to do so and if you will all return with Dorothy and me to the Land of Oz, where Ozma will make you welcome, I will ask Glinda to try to break this enchantment."

This was willingly agreed to, for they all

welcomed the chance to visit the famous Land of Oz. So they bade good-bye to King Kaliko, whom Dorothy warned not to be wicked any more if he could help it, and the entire party returned over the Magic Carpet to the Land of Oz. They filled the Red Wagon, which was still waiting for them, pretty full; but the Sawhorse didn't mind that and with wonderful speed carried them safely to the Emerald City.

Ozma's Banquet

CHAPTER 22

OZMA had seen in her
Magic Picture the liber-
ation of Inga's parents
and the departure of the
entire party for the Em-
erald City, so with her usual hospitality she
ordered a splendid banquet prepared and invited all her quaint friends who were then in
the Emerald City to be present that evening to
meet the strangers who were to become her
guests.

Glinda, also, in her wonderful Record Book
had learned of the events that had taken place
in the caverns of the Nome King and she became especially interested in the enchantment
of the Prince of Boboland. So she hastily prepared several of her most powerful charms and

then summoned her flock of sixteen white
storks, which swiftly bore her to Ozma's palace.
She arrived there before the Red Wagon did
and was warmly greeted by the girl Ruler.

Realizing that the costume of Queen Garee
of Pingaree must have become sadly worn and
frayed, owing to her hardships and adventures,
Ozma ordered a royal outfit prepared for the
good Queen and had it laid in her chamber
ready for her to put on as soon as she arrived, so
she would not be shamed at the banquet. New
costumes were also provided for King Kitticut
and King Rinkitink and Prince Inga, all cut and
made and embellished in the elaborate and becoming style then prevalent in the Land of Oz,
and as soon as the party arrived at the palace
Ozma's guests were escorted by her servants to
their rooms, that they might bathe and dress
themselves.

Glinda the Sorceress and the Wizard of Oz
took charge of Bilbil the goat and went to a
private room where they were not likely to be
interrupted. Glinda first questioned Bilbil long
and earnestly about the manner of his enchantment and the ceremony that had been used by
the magician who enchanted him. At first Bilbil
protested that he did not want to be restored to
his natural shape, saying that he had been forever disgraced in the eyes of his people and of
the entire world by being obliged to exist as a

scrawny, scraggly goat. But Glinda pointed out that any person who incurred the enmity of a wicked magician was liable to suffer a similar fate, and assured him that his misfortune would make him better beloved by his subjects when he returned to them freed from his dire enchantment.

Bilbil was finally convinced of the truth of this assertion and agreed to submit to the experiments of Glinda and the Wizard, who knew they had a hard task before them and were not at all sure they could succeed. We know that Glinda is the most complete mistress of magic who has ever existed, and she was wise enough to guess that the clever but evil magician who had enchanted Prince Bobo had used a spell that would puzzle any ordinary wizard or sorcerer to break; therefore she had given the matter much shrewd thought and hoped she had conceived a plan that would succeed. But because she was not positive of success she would have no one present at the incantation except her assistant, the Wizard of Oz.

First she transformed Bilbil the goat into a lamb, and this was done quite easily. Next she transformed the lamb into an ostrich, giving it two legs and feet instead of four. Then she tried to transform the ostrich into the original Prince Bobo, but this incantation was an utter failure. Glinda was not discouraged, however, but by a

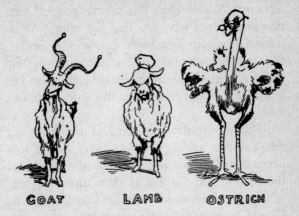

GOAT   LAMB   OSTRICH

powerful spell transformed the ostrich into a tottenhot—which is a lower form of a man. Then the tottenhot was transformed into a mifket, which was a great step in advance and, finally, Glinda transformed the mifket into a handsome young man, tall and shapely, who fell on his knees before the great Sorceress and gratefully kissed her hand, admitting that he had now recovered his proper shape and was indeed Prince Bobo of Boboland.

This process of magic, successful though it was in the end, had required so much time that the banquet was now awaiting their presence. Bobo was already dressed in princely raiment and although he seemed very much humbled by his recent lowly condition, they finally persuaded him to join the festivities.

TOTTENHOT

PRINCE

NIFKET

When Rinkitink saw that his goat had now become a Prince, he did not know whether to be sorry or glad, for he felt that he would miss the companionship of the quarrelsome animal he had so long been accustomed to ride upon, while at the same time he rejoiced that poor Bilbil had come to his own again.

Prince Bobo humbly begged Rinkitink's forgiveness for having been so disagreeable to him, at times, saying that the nature of a goat had influenced him and the surly disposition he had shown was a part of his enchantment. But the jolly King assured the Prince that he had really enjoyed Bilbil's grumpy speeches and forgave him readily. Indeed, they all discovered the young Prince Bobo to be an exceedingly courteous and pleasant person, although he was somewhat reserved and dignified.

BETSY   TROT

Ah, but it was a great feast that Ozma served in her gorgeous banquet hall that night and everyone was as happy as could be. The Shaggy Man was there, and so was Jack Pumpkinhead and the Tin Woodman and Cap'n Bill. Beside Princess Dorothy sat Tiny Trot and Betsy Bobbin, and the three little girls were almost as sweet to look upon as was Ozma, who sat at the head of her table and outshone all her guests in loveliness.

King Rinkitink was delighted with the quaint people of Oz and laughed and joked with the tin man and the pumpkin-headed man and found Cap'n Bill a very agreeable companion. But what amused the jolly King most were the animal guests, which Ozma always invited to her banquets and seated at a table by themselves, where they talked and chatted together as people do

OZMA   DOROTHY

but were served the sort of food their natures required. The Hungry Tiger and Cowardly Lion and the Glass Cat were much admired by Rinkitink, but when he met a mule named Hank, which Betsy Bobbin had brought to Oz, the King found the creature so comical that he laughed and chuckled until his friends thought he would choke. Then while the banquet was still in progress, Rinkitink composed and sang a song to the mule and they all joined in the chorus, which was something like this:

"It's very queer how big an ear
   Is worn by Mr. Donkey;
And yet I fear he could not hear
   If it were on a monkey.

'Tis thick and strong and broad and long
  And also very hairy;
It's quite becoming to our Hank
  But might disgrace a fairy!"

This song was received with so much enthusiasm that Rinkitink was prevailed upon to sing another. They gave him a little time to compose the rhyme, which he declared would be better if he could devote a month or two to its composition, but the sentiment he expressed was so admirable that no one criticized the song or the manner in which the jolly little King sang it.

Dorothy wrote down the words on a piece of paper, and here they are:

"We're merry comrades all, to-night,
Because we've won a gallant fight
  And conquered all our foes.
We're not afraid of anything,
So let us gayly laugh and sing
  Until we seek repose.

"We've all our grateful hearts can wish;
King Gos has gone to feed the fish,
  Queen Cor has gone, as well;
King Kitticut has found his own,
Prince Bobo soon will have a throne
  Relieved of magic spell.

"So let's forget the horrid strife
That fell upon our peaceful life
   And caused distress and pain;
For very soon across the sea
We'll all be sailing merrily
   To Pingaree again."

The Pearl Kingdom

CHAPTER 23

IT was unfortunate that
the famous Scarecrow—
the most popular person
in all Oz, next to Ozma
—was absent at the time
of the banquet, for he happened just then to be
making one of his trips through the country;
but the Scarecrow had a chance later to meet
Rinkitink and Inga and the King and Queen of
Pingaree and Prince Bobo, for the party remained several weeks at the Emerald City, where
they were royally entertained, and where both
the gentle Queen Garee and the noble King
Kitticut recovered much of their good spirits and
composure and tried to forget their dreadful ex-
periences.

At last, however, the King and Queen desired

to return to their own Pingaree, as they longed to be with their people again and see how well they had rebuilt their homes. Inga also was anxious to return, although he had been very happy in Oz, and King Rinkitink, who was happy anywhere except at Gilgad, decided to go with his former friends to Pingaree. As for Prince Bobo, he had become so greatly attached to King Rinkitink that he was loth to leave him.

On a certain day they all bade good-bye to Ozma and Dorothy and Glinda and the Wizard and all their good friends in Oz, and were driven in the Red Wagon to the edge of the Deadly Desert, which they crossed safely on the Magic Carpet. They then made their way across the Nome Kingdom and the Wheeler Country, where no one molested them, to the shores of the Nonestic Ocean. There they found the boat with the silver lining still lying undisturbed on the beach.

There were no important adventures during the trip and on their arrival at the pearl kingdom they were amazed at the beautiful appearance of the island they had left in ruins. All the houses of the people had been rebuilt and were prettier than before, with green lawns before them and flower gardens in the back yards. The marble towers of King Kitticut's new palace were very striking and impressive, while the palace itself proved far more magnificent than it

had been before the warriors from Regos destroyed it.

Nikobob had been very active and skillful in directing all this work, and he had also built a pretty cottage for himself, not far from the King's palace, and there Inga found Zella, who was living very happy and contented in her new home. Not only had Nikobob accomplished all this in a comparatively brief space of time, but he had started the pearl fisheries again and when King Kitticut returned to Pingaree he found a quantity of fine pearls already in the royal treasury.

So pleased was Kitticut with the good judgment, industry and honesty of the former charcoal-burner of Regos, that he made Nikobob his Lord High Chamberlain and put him in charge of the pearl fisheries and all the business matters of the island kingdom.

They all settled down very comfortably in the new palace and the Queen gathered her maids about her once more and set them to work embroidering new draperies for the royal throne. Inga placed the three Magic Pearls in their silken bag and again deposited them in the secret cavity under the tiled flooring of the banquet hall, where they could be quickly secured if danger ever threatened the now prosperous island.

King Rinkitink occupied a royal guest chamber built especially for his use and seemed in no hurry to leave his friends in Pingaree. The fat little King had to walk wherever he went and so missed Bilbil more and more; but he seldom walked far and he was so fond of Prince Bobo that he never regretted Bilbil's disenchantment.

Indeed, the jolly monarch was welcome to remain forever in Pingaree, if he wished to, for his merry disposition set smiles on the faces of all his friends and made everyone near him as jolly as he was himself. When King Kitticut was not too busy with affairs of state he loved to join his guest and listen to his brother monarch's songs and stories. For he found Rinkitink to be, with all his careless disposition, a shrewd philosopher, and in talking over their adventures one day the King of Gilgad said:

"The beauty of life is its sudden changes. No one knows what is going to happen next, and so we are constantly being surprised and entertained. The many ups and downs should not discourage us, for if we are down, we know that a change is coming and we will go up again; while those who are up are almost certain to go down. My grandfather had a song which well expresses this and if you will listen I will sing it."

"Of course I will listen to your song," returned Kitticut, "for it would be impolite not to."

So Rinkitink sang his grandfather's song:

The Pearl Kingdom

"A mighty King once ruled the land—
   But now he's baking pies.
A pauper, on the other hand,
   Is ruling, strong and wise.

A tiger once in jungles raged—
   But now he's in a zoo;
A lion, captive-born and caged,
   Now roams the forest through.

A man once slapped a poor boy's pate
   And made him weep and wail.
The boy became a magistrate
   And put the man in jail.

A sunny day succeeds the night;
   It's summer—then it snows!
Right oft goes wrong and wrong comes right,
   As ev'ry wise man knows."

The Captive King

CHAPTER 24

ONE morning, just as
the royal party was fin-
ishing breakfast, a serv-
ant came running to say
that a great fleet of boats
was approaching the island from the south. King
Kitticut sprang up at once, in great alarm, for
he had much cause to fear strange boats. The
others quickly followed him to the shore to see
what invasion might be coming upon them.

Inga was there with the first, and Nikobob
and Zella soon joined the watchers. And presently, while all were gazing eagerly at the approaching fleet, King Rinkitink suddenly cried
out:

"Get your pearls, Prince Inga—get them
quick!"

"Are these our enemies, then?" asked the boy, looking with surprise upon the fat little King, who had begun to tremble violently.

"They are my people of Gilgad!" answered Rinkitink, wiping a tear from his eye. "I recognize my royal standards flying from the boats. So, please, dear Inga, get out your pearls to protect me!"

"What can you fear at the hands of your own subjects?" asked Kitticut, astonished.

But before his frightened guest could answer the question Prince Bobo, who was standing beside his friend, gave an amused laugh and said:

"You are caught at last, dear Rinkitink. Your people will take you home again and oblige you to reign as King."

Rinkitink groaned aloud and clasped his hands together with a gesture of despair, an attitude so comical that the others could scarcely forbear laughing.

But now the boats were landing upon the beach. They were fifty in number, beautifully decorated and upholstered and rowed by men clad in the gay uniforms of the King of Gilgad. One splended boat had a throne of gold in the center, over which was draped the King's royal robe of purple velvet, embroidered with gold buttercups.

Rinkitink shuddered when he saw this throne; but now a tall man, handsomely dressed, approached and knelt upon the grass before his King, while all the other occupants of the boats shouted joyfully and waved their plumed hats in the air.

"Thanks to our good fortune," said the man who kneeled, "we have found Your Majesty at last!"

"Pinkerbloo," answered Rinkitink sternly, "I must have you hanged, for thus finding me against my will."

"You think so now, Your Majesty, but you will never do it," returned Pinkerbloo, rising and kissing the King's hand.

"Why won't I?" asked Rinkitink.

"Because you are much too tender-hearted, Your Majesty."

"It may be—it may be," agreed Rinkitink, sadly. "It is one of my greatest failings. But what chance brought you here, my Lord Pinkerbloo?"

"We have searched for you everywhere, sire, and all the people of Gilgad have been in despair since you so mysteriously disappeared. We could not appoint a new King, because we did not know but that you still lived; so we set out to find you, dead or alive. After visiting many islands of the Nonestic Ocean we at last thought of Pingaree, from where come the precious pearls; and now our faithful quest has been rewarded."

"And what now?" asked Rinkitink.

"Now, Your Majesty, you must come home with us, like a good and dutiful King, and rule over your people," declared the man in a firm voice.

"I will not."

"But you must—begging Your Majesty's pardon for the contradiction."

"Kitticut," cried poor Rinkitink, "you must save me from being captured by these, my subjects. What! must I return to Gilgad and be forced to reign in splendid state when I much prefer to eat and sleep and sing in my own quiet way? They will make me sit in a throne three hours a day and listen to dry and tedious affairs of state; and I must stand up for hours at the court receptions, till I get corns on my heels; and forever must I listen to tiresome speeches and endless petitions and complaints!"

"But someone must do this, Your Majesty," said Pinkerbloo respectfully, "and since you were born to be our King you cannot escape your duty."

"'Tis a horrid fate!" moaned Rinkitink. "I would die willingly, rather than be a King—if it did not hurt so terribly to die."

"You will find it much more comfortable to reign than to die, although I fully appreciate Your Majesty's difficult position and am truly sorry for you," said Pinkerbloo.

King Kitticut had listened to this conversation

thoughtfully, so now he said to his friend:

"The man is right, dear Rinkitink. It is your duty to reign, since fate has made you a King, and I see no honorable escape for you. I shall grieve to lose your companionship, but I feel the separation cannot be avoided."

Rinkitink sighed.

"Then," said he, turning to Lord Pinkerbloo, "in three days I will depart with you for Gilgad; but during those three days I propose to feast and make merry with my good friend King Kitticut."

Then all the people of Gilgad shouted with delight and eagerly scrambled ashore to take their part in the festival.

Those three days were long remembered in Pingaree, for never—before nor since—has such feasting and jollity been known upon that island. Rinkitink made the most of his time and everyone laughed and sang with him by day and by night.

Then, at last, the hour of parting arrived and the King of Gilgad and Ruler of the Dominion of Rinkitink was escorted by a grand procession to his boat and seated upon his golden throne. The rowers of the fifty boats paused, with their glittering oars pointed into the air like gigantic uplifted sabres, while the people of Pingaree—men, women and children—stood upon the shore shouting a royal farewell to the jolly King.

Then came a sudden hush, while Rinkitink stood up and, with a bow to those assembled to witness his departure, sang the following song, which he had just composed for the occasion.

"Farewell, dear Isle of Pingaree—
The fairest land in all the sea!
No living mortals, kings or churls,
Would scorn to wear thy precious pearls.

"King Kitticut, 'tis with regret
I'm forced to say farewell; and yet
Abroad no longer can I roam
When fifty boats would drag me home.

"Good-bye, my Prince of Pingaree;
A noble King some time you'll be
And long and wisely may you reign
And never face a foe again!"

They cheered him from the shore; they cheered him from the boats; and then all the oars of the fifty boats swept downward with a single motion and dipped their blades into the purple-hued waters of the Nonestic Ocean.

As the boats shot swiftly over the ripples of the sea Rinkitink turned to Prince Bobo, who had decided not to desert his former master and his present friend, and asked anxiously:

"How did you like that song, Bilbil—I mean Bobo? Is it a masterpiece, do you think?"

And Bobo replied with a smile:

"Like all your songs, dear Rinkitink, the sentiment far excels the poetry."

DEL REY BOOKS invites you to the wonderful world of OZ

Enchanting
fantasies
from

DEL REY BOOKS